Midnight & Mistletoe

AMANDA KIMBERLEY

About Midnight & Mistletoe

The heart of a man is through his bite.

When prim and proper Priya Pant started work at the Odd Duck, she expected a professional kitchen, given the man that hired her. But what she got from Braden Boss was just plain fowl!

Hurting for money and longing for a chance to redeem herself from a former billionaire life, she tries to ignore Boss's bad-boy behavior, but the more she tries to maintain her measured distance from the man, the more he wants to stir the pot.

Braden Boss has always gotten what he wanted and has done what pleases him. Vampires with money and status possess that kind of privilege.

The problem was that no matter what he wanted out of life—whether it was fortune, fame, or devotion from all his television groupies—he wasn't happy.

After living four centuries, any vampire expects to run into a slump of boredom. But Braden was looking for the one ingredient he never seemed to find in any other method of pleasure. He wanted love. Or at least, Priya, the sous-chef he hired for her perky breasts, proved he should toss out his old recipes and whip up love from scratch.

For my readers, no matter what you celebrate, Solstice, Yule, Lita, Bodhi, Hanukkah, Christmas, Three Kings, Posadas Navidenas, Zarathosht Diso, or Kwanzaa, Yom Kippur, Ashura, to name a few, I hope y'all have the happiest of holidays!

Chapter One

NEW BEGINNINGS

Priya tried to braid her hair again for the fourth time, but she still couldn't get the frizz fest to behave itself.

"It's no use. I'm going to have to jump in the shower and drench it."

It was the first day of her new life, and everything had to be perfect since she'd be working with *"the"* Braden Boss, a highly successful chef with his own TV show on The Food Channel. She wasn't horribly keen on having had to use her womanly wiles on the man to get the job, but her daddy always said, 'If you've got it, flaunt it.' And her triple D cup size surely became a definitive flaunting mechanism with this man.

Three years ago, she wouldn't have had to stoop so low to allow her physical features to speak for her successes. Her money and fame in the business world made her a respected woman back then. But now, after everything she'd suffered, including her own dignity ripped from her, she found herself starting over. Sadly, she had less than when she was fresh out of college, which proved to be the worst low of her life. Because now? Now she needed to be content with playing second fiddle as a sous-chef to one of the most famous culinary brilliants in the business today. Not that she couldn't share the spotlight. She was good at that, but given what she knew about Boss, he wouldn't share it —he'd hog it.

The braid finally took shape after she drenched her hair, and she secured it with a hair tie before she let out a tremendous sigh.

"Please, my dear Lord, let me get through today with little to no problems. It will be bad enough to swallow my pride for the next 10 hours because the last thing I need is an ogling boss or a botched dinner."

She put on a little foundation, blush, and mascara —not wanting to look as if she just came off the runway since what she had on was distracting enough. The man—at least during the interview proved incorrigible, only hiring her for her perky assets, so she didn't need to prove him right by gussying herself up to the nines. He never looked north of her chest during the hour-long interview. That alone convinced her the tabloids had been right. He was a billionaire bad-boy who only had a serious relationship with his coffee maker. Of course, she had something in common with his Keurig. The man knew how to push her buttons.

She grabbed her purse and keys and headed out the door. The drive to The Odd Duck wasn't far from her apartment via the highway. But come winter, she'd have to leave her house two hours early during a snow "storm" to use the back roads if she had any hopes of getting there on time. Southerners weren't exactly known for being able to drive in inclement weather. Two inches of snow here would compare to a blizzard up in New England—at least according to her cousins from New York City. Texas though? They shut everything down because they can't treat the highways with massive car pileups. And she was not looking forward to January and February, which were only a few short weeks away. It was almost unheard of to land a job in the restaurant field so close to the holidays.

Sure, waitstaff positions were always open, but typically not management. Not that Priya needed the money for Christmas gifts, most of her family was long since buried. Still, since her divorce, she made it a point to look forward to treating herself with a lavish Christmas gift. She felt she deserved it after the hell her ex put her through, and she wasn't going to back down on such a thing this year. It was the first year she could use money from a paycheck instead of her bank account, and she would take pride in herself for accomplishing so much in such little time. She knew no one else at her age that had to start over. Sure, some people go back to school and change careers after retirement, but she was far from her golden years, and she wasn't about to live off her dividends alone. No. She wanted a sense of accomplishment just like anyone else did in their barely thirties did.

She found a parking space a lengthy distance away from the restaurant under a streetlight and pulled in. Once she turned the car off, she let out a long breath to steady her nerves before opening the door. This was like her first job-first day jitters all over again. She slowly placed both feet on the ground and locked her car, trying to stamp out some of her nerves before proceeding toward the entrance. Her stomach did a few backflips as she tried to put one foot in front of the other to make it to the door.

Once through the threshold, a hostess greeted her. Her eyes were half-mast and sunken in, and the haphazard eyeliner she applied appeared as if it was from the night before. The bags under her eyes were the most prominent feature of her pale face. She looked overworked and overloaded. Priya scanned the restaurant to see if the rest of the staff was just as tired and most likely hungover, and to her astonishment, it appeared they all were. This was clearly something she needed to change if the place was ever going to appear upscale and professional. The Odd Duck wasn't a chain restaurant with a revolving door of employees. It was established with the intent of being a leading dining experience from ingredients provided by local farmers.

The minute she knew she was interviewing with Boss, Priya began dreaming about Michelin Stars—not that The Odd Duck was even thinking about upscale. They started out humbly like any other restaurant with an unusual yet awesome goal. They only used ingredients from local farmers so they could provide a local unique experience, something Priya could get behind. Now that he had hired her, she wanted the best recognition she could get for the restaurant and for Brayden. Priya cleared her throat, plastered her biggest Southern smile, and asked where the boss was. The hostess's eyes widened.

"We don't call Mr. Boss 'the boss.'" She said with air quotes. "He absolutely hates that. Just a fair warning since this is your first day, Ms.?"

"Priya Pant, but please, call me Priya! I'm not one for such formalities among adults I work with." She bounced out the words as she extended her hand to the hostess, whose lips seemed to thin to nonexistence by the minute. The woman, who wasn't much older than Priya, flicked her eyes to the extended hand and then back to Priya's gaze.

"Um, you might want to rethink what you've got going on as a first impression. Because the formality of your name is about the only thing respected around here. Again—fair warning. Come on. I'll show you to the kitchen." She said as she turned on her heel and motioned for Priya to follow.

Priya lowered her hand and frowned. She was barely in the door and was already having one of the worst days of her life.

Who doesn't shake hands? Clearly, none of them here! That needs to change.

Priya sucked in a breath as the hostess opened the door to the kitchen. She then motioned for Priya to walk in. Priya's brow furrowed as the hostess turned to walk away.

"Aren't you going to take me to Mr. Boss?"

"Hell no! I stay as far away from the kitchen as I can. No offense, lady? But good luck to you! Maybe I'll see you outside for a smoke break. We like to have bitch sessions out there. Of course, that's if you survive that long."

Priya narrowed her eyes. "I don't smoke."

The hostess laughed loud and long. It almost sounded like a cackle.

"Well, you may not be a smoker now, but I predict you probably will start up soon! Mr. Boss isn't exactly the easiest person to get along with. I figured I'd give you a fair warning since you didn't figure that out from my candor at the door."

Priya shook her head at the clearly deranged woman. There was little she could do to fix the girl's attitude this early in her sous-chef career at The Odd Duck, but she vowed she'd try. She sucked in a long breath and headed into the kitchen.

A loud clanging filled the air, followed by a mouth so foul she wondered if the vegetables were still fresh.

"Son of a bitch! This sauce tastes like absolute ass! A five-year-old can do better! Make it again, God damn it! And this time—season it before you put that shit in the pan! You graduated from Cornell, for Christ's sake! I expect the best from you, for fuck's sake!"

Priya palmed her reddening cheeks. In all her years of growing up as a minister's daughter, no more than two swear words passed her daddy's lips. And now, her new employer, Braden Boss, said more explicit remarks in two minutes than she had ever heard in her entire lifetime.

Jesus, Mary, and Joseph! What have I gotten myself into?

Braden looked up from the now crying young prep woman and locked his eyes on Priya.

"Thank God you are here! At least someone with an ounce of talent can help me with this fucking train wreck!" He said as he tossed his hands in the air. "Come with me to my office, and we'll go over some itineraries for today's specials. After that, I will have you work with Ms. Fucking Prima Donna right here, so my recipes come out the way I intended them to and not with an added flavor spin that sucks monkey balls. The only way for this restaurant to succeed is for everyone to fucking execute the dishes properly!" He said this in a low growl through gritted teeth before motioning Priya to another area of the kitchen with a door.

Priya stood frozen in her stance. Her knees locked as she tried to will them to move. She did not know that she'd be walking into *Hell's Kitchen* with the Devil reincarnate as her boss, but Priya did get a few things as she was willing her feet to think for themselves. First, she had to force her legs to walk fast because he was already halfway across the kitchen in two strides. Two, she would not give this heathen the satisfaction of watching her burn under the collar. And three, paying for the roof over her head depended on her compromising with this Lucifer. Daddy always taught her about signing her soul away. But clearly, Daddy never met *the* Boss that could accomplish that just by signing her paychecks.

Somehow, somehow, she could put one shaking foot in front of the other and make it to his office.

"Shut the door." He motioned to her as she stepped through it.

He locked on her eyes, but as soon as she sat down in the empty seat opposite him, his eyes went south. Priya frowned at the gesture. Sure, she stooped to a new level of stupid with getting hired, but that didn't mean she had to take his ogling daily at work. He should be more of a professional gentleman, but clearly—he didn't get the memo.

"So, Ms. Perky, let's talk about the specials for today." He said with a smile, eyes still locked on her chest.

Priya bent down slightly in her chair to meet his gaze and waved a hand in front of his eyes.

"Hi. First off, my eyes are north of where you are looking. Second, it's Priya—not perky." She said as she crossed her arms over her chest.

It didn't do much to cover up her enormous triple-D cups, but she certainly didn't want to get the attention she had been in his office for the last few minutes.

He chuckled.

"Whatever you say, Ms. Perky."

Priya let out a huff.

Braden cleared his throat and lowered his gaze to the floor before continuing. "Sorry, Ms. Priya. So, let's get down to business and pick from these four for today's and tomorrow's specials. I was thinking either quail stuffed with fresh figs and prosciutto or quail in rose petal sauce for the first choice and for the second either smoky citrus butter-baked redfish or mustard-maple roasted salmon." He said as he spread some notes onto the desk in front of her. His fingertips brushed her hand slightly as she reached for one page of notes and an electric heat surged through the tips of her fingers that traveled right down to her core.

There was no denying that Braden was attractive with his luscious dark and wavy locks and chestnut brown eyes. His solid forearms and citrus, musky scent drove her to the point of insanity too. But no amount of crazy would be worth an attraction to the foul-mouthed buffoon. She shook her head in protest of her body's reaction and crossed her legs to stop her libido from singing any amount of praise to the gorgeous god before her. He was her employer, and that was that.

"Well, my specialty is Italian and Southern foods. I'd love to work with the prosciutto and fig recipe because it sounds fun and flavorful. As far as the fish goes—wild salmon is in season now through August, so we should take advantage of the mustard-maple recipe. Even the maple syrup will be delicious now because it is also in season. The redfish recipe sounds mouth-watering, but I'd wait till August for that one.

Perhaps we can do smoked citrus for a salmon dish for tomorrow instead?"

Braden smiled from ear to ear. "Apparently, I was right about you being sharp. I threw in the red herring —or in this case—the redfish to see if you knew what was seasonal. I've always found fish should be in season for a perfect meal because it just tastes better." His eyes met hers for the first time since they walked into his office, and she could see they were twinkling with delight as he talked about food. It was the first time he appeared human instead of a horny bastard.

"I know we talked briefly in the interview, but I never got to ask what your favorite dish is to prepare."

He was clearly searching, and Priya was tongue-tied. No man should look that gorgeous! It should be a crime against humanity. Of course, his potty mouth left much to be desired, and she focused on that to get the wheels in her brain to move. Still, what could she possibly say to impress this famous chef?

"Well, in all honesty, it would have to be manicotti." She blurted out the statement almost without thinking it over. She drew out her pronunciation of manicotti in an Italian/New York/Southern drawl. "My grandma made them from scratch every Thanksgiving, and I make them on special occasions in her memory. I do the same with lasagna, too—even though she didn't make that as much."

His eyes brightened again. He got up from behind his desk and reached out to cup Priya's cheeks. Priya shot up from her chair. Sure, she thought the guy was a hornball, but she never thought he'd touch her this brazenly in his own office, at which any point someone could enter. They were nearly a breath apart, and Priya sucked in as much air as she dared through her slightly parted lips. He couldn't know he had this effect on her because she wouldn't allow it.

"Priya, I didn't care about the dish you'd tell me. All I cared about was the passion behind it. I knew my gut was right about hiring you." He said while he pressed his lips on both of her cheeks and made a soft smacking sound. They were so buttery smooth, and she barely realized he was kissing her until he met her gaze again. She tried to recoup her look of horror, but she wasn't doing very well in hiding it. "Sorry! I don't mean to make you uncomfortable. It's just that you remind me of my family. They were all chefs and all from Europe. I'm sure you know it's customary to greet each other by kissing cheeks."

"Really? You didn't care about the dish?" She found her hands cupping both of his that still cradled her face. She blinked a second longer than she needed to as Priya moved into his touch, but only slightly before she corrected herself. *He's your boss, Priya! Stop panting over him!* "And no, the European greeting isn't uncomfortable for me. I'm literally second-gen off of the boat. My grandparents were the first to arrive here off Ellis Island. After growing up in my family and spending a summer abroad, I'm used to the warm welcome in Italy and Spain. My dad's side has been here far longer. He's from India originally." Her eyes widened at her own realization of surprise and shock intermixing her feelings at his gesture. She didn't want such closeness with the man because of who he was, yet her body hummed the instant he touched her.

"Yes, my family is mostly from Europe and mostly Italy, though I have some India descent in my family tree on his side, too." He said as he lowered his hands and placed them in the pockets of his skin-tight black jeans.

God, how she wished to be those hands touching his skin through that thin layer of fabric on his thighs. *Priya! Don't, girl! It's barely an hour into your first day!*

"Sounds nice. Mine were mostly from Italy, too."

"I wish I could have them here for the holidays. Unfortunately, they are all deceased."

"I'm sorry to hear that. It's always hard when our loved ones have passed. I've had my fair share of family members dying these past few years, too. There aren't that many of mine left either. I've got some cousins on my grandfather's brother's side, and that's the side from India. But that's about it."

"Yes, and sadly, you can't do anything except live on without them."

"True." Priya lowered her gaze.

Not knowing what more to say, she quickly changed the subject. This was the first time she met and connected with her boss, and she'd be damned if she screwed this up. She had to get him to like her; talking about dead relatives would not cut it.

"So, have we decided on quail stuffed with prosciutto and figs?"

"I think so. Come back to the kitchen, and I'll show you how I make and plate it." He said as he patted her shoulder and smiled.

Another wave of energy surged through her body as his hand patted her shoulder, and she swore her stomach did a backflip.

They both worked in relative silence in large part in the now all too massive kitchen for the first few minutes as they diced up some onions and garlic. To Priya's surprise, it was an extremely comfortable quiet between them. Usually, when getting to know a coworker, she'd fill the time with idle chat, but this time was different. She didn't feel a need for it. He didn't swear up a firestorm as he had earlier in the morning, which was a welcome relief. But he didn't talk all that much either. However, he did tower over her shoulder as she seasoned the quail with salt and pepper on her cutlery board. She wasn't one to use more than the pinch her ancestors told her to use. Sure, some of them would argue as she grabbed the seasoning between her fingers. But in the end, they all seemed to celebrate once she gingerly salted and peppered her meal. A rush of heat shot through her as he gently tapped her on her forearm.

"Very good. Now rub the meat with this herbal poultry mix and butter like this." The tone was as soft as the touch of his hands over hers.

"Make sure you get every curve—I mean cranny. Rub every part of that thing, so it browns well."

She laughed internally after she let out a shaky breath. Clearly, she wasn't the only one moved by the love they were making in this kitchen.

Priya! Stop it, girl. No sexy thoughts while you make food!

"Yes, sir." She had to say something and thought it was best to jest with a cheeky smile.

"Here," He handed her the figs and prosciutto to place inside the bird's cavity.

His hand grazed hers again, sending another course of electric heat through her arm and traveling straight to her core.

"Thanks." She directed her gaze at the bird in a desperate attempt to avoid eye contact.

"That looks beautiful."

"Thanks. I think it looks good, too."

"The quail?" He whispered in her ear as he bent over her.

"Yes, the quail. What did you think I meant?" She asked as heat rushed to her cheeks when she turned to meet his gaze.

His lips turned into a broad smile.

"I'm asking if you could pass me the quail so I can place it in the oven, but if you must know, that dish isn't the only beautiful thing in this kitchen."

She swallowed hard before handing him the dutch oven that contained the quail, and he placed it in the oven. She quickly busied herself with chopping some lettuce for the side salads they were pairing with the quail.

The aroma of the quail browning beautifully in the oven touched their noses after an hour of baking. Braden pulled them out and smiled as he turned to her.

"Smells and looks like perfection." He said while he made up a plate. "I'll leave you to plating yours as I have shown you here." He said as he started wiping his hands. "You can sample these since this was a practice plate. I'll catch you before the dinner rush. I have a taping to do for the show and will be out for the rest of the afternoon."

Priya smiled at him briefly before getting to work on plating the dish. She watched him leave the kitchen. It was bittersweet to see him go because even though his backside was genuinely exquisite, she had to admit that a part of her wanted him to stay. Cooking up something a little more with her than just a dish was looking to be more on her menu than she cared to admit to herself. And she blushed at the thought of feeling that way about her boss.

Having spent more time with him proved he wasn't as intimidating of a person as she initially thought he was. Still, she was happy that he wouldn't be breathing down her neck for the next few hours, giving her the freedom to walk about the kitchen without brushing against his hard body. The back of her neck began to sweat just thinking about how many times his hips touched hers while chopping away. And the reprieve would give her something else. It would be the chance she needed to build a rapport with the others in the restaurant. Especially that crazy hostess and the poor prep chef who was still sulking in a dark corner of the kitchen.

Priya knew she needed to get the employees to see Braden's good side. If they could see that, they might be more cheerful and professional while on the job. And that, and not so much the food, was Priya's focus for this budding restaurant.

Still, her long-term goals would be pointless if she didn't perfect his execution. She looked up from her plate and compared it to his, which looked identical. She was pleased with herself right down to the carefully placed herbal garnish.

"C—can you show me what I did wrong?" Said a shaky voice to her right.

Priya looked up from the plates and saw the woman Braden had yelled at earlier. Her blue eyes were bloodshot and puffy from an apparent marathon crying session. Some of her short black hair clung to her cheeks, which were stained with tears.

"Sure. Why don't you get more quail, and we can start a new batch from scratch? I'm Priya, Priya Pant, by the way."

"Donna. Donna Brightman." Said the woman as she nodded with a weak smile.

Donna looked at what Priya was doing and followed until their plates mimicked each other.

"Perfect, Donna!" Priya said with a smile.

The kitchen door flung open. Braden walked through and headed straight towards them both. He looked at both plates, sampled them both, and nodded approval.

"Thanks for setting Donna straight, Priya."

Donna lowered her head and tiptoed to the prep station in the kitchen's corner to start on the asparagus for the salmon side dish. She let out a sigh. Braden followed Donna with his gaze as she walked over to the cutting board. He shook his head slightly and then turned his eyes to Priya.

"What's wrong with her? She's acting like I killed her cat." Braden said in a loud whisper.

"She's still upset about this morning."

"Why? It was a mistake—she corrected it, and we moved on."

"Braden, do you not remember your tone and all the foul language you used with her this morning?"

"Oh, for Christ's sake! I swear all the time. That's just who I am."

"It's an unbecoming tone for an employer." Said Priya as she frowned and shook her head.

"Oh, please, is Little Miss Prissy Priya going to tell me the error of my ways?"

Braden crossed his arms and puffed out his chest as he chuckled. Priya didn't want a choral repeat of this morning, so she narrowed her eyes and crossed her own arms in retort.

"For your information, my daddy was a preacher, and he taught us we didn't need to swear to get our point across to others. He also taught us not to name-call. You do realize that name-calling is a form of bullying, and you, sir, are acting like a child with all your elementary school comments." Priya let out a puff of breath. She couldn't believe she was sticking up for herself and the employees she and her boss shared this early in the game. But as his eyes softened to amusement levels, she grew angrier. "You know, I really thought I was getting through to you earlier when we were cooking the quail together. I guess I was wrong." She let out another breath. "It's like you've got a Jekyll and Hyde syndrome going on or something."

Braden's eyes widened, and his lips curled up before he let out a chuckle. This one was heartier than his first.

"Wow! I didn't think I hired a true Southern belle. This is going to be interesting." He laughed again before turning on his heel to head towards his office. "Very interesting, indeed. Hopefully, you can keep up with this Texas kitchen heat, Ms. Priya."

"What's that supposed to mean?"

Braden laughed again before closing the door to his office. She desperately wanted to run after him, giving him more pieces of her mind. The man clearly needed a good tongue lashing because he forgot the manners his momma, bless her heart, taught him. Of all the times she'd used the phrase, this was most likely the first time she was using it out of sympathy for a woman she only knew through the tabloids and media. A regal and proud woman whose eyes lit up with adoration whenever the papzz interviewed her about Brayden as a child. After a few seconds had passed and she slowed her breathing, she decided against following him. The only certainty of an action like that was her getting fired. And now, more than ever, she wanted to keep this job. If for no other reason, she was determined to keep it to show Mr. Bossypants that he couldn't get her goat!

Chapter Two

SOUTHERN COMFORT

Braden had come into work far too early again, and this time he did it without a coffee in hand. It's always a dangerous move to go without it, and not because of being tired and needing the caffeine to feel more alive. He was a vampire, so there was no need for a jolt to awaken. Being immortal meant never tiring and never needing to sleep. But the need for caffeine was two-fold. One, it made him feel more capable of functioning in the kitchen. The sweet nectar was satisfying and paired well with blood, should he need to conceal his thirst around the humans he employed. And two, bringing the cup to his mouth has helped squelch some of the choice words he has wished to express to the idiots he works with frequently.

He wished he'd stayed home a little longer this morning because the 18 hours spent yesterday taping for his show, "Cooking Like The Boss," was excruciating. It was mostly a waste of a day on the set, and he also wasted what little time he had yesterday to pick the specials for the week. Usually, a long day wouldn't faze him, but working with a cameraman that couldn't get the right angles to save his career proved beyond difficult.

In the cameraman's defense, he was fresh out of college, but they should have never trusted that guy with a show ranking number one on the Food Channel. The taping was so bad that no amount of duct tape would fix the blatant errors. Though Braden wondered if the beautiful invention could muffle the sound of the whining coming from the college puke every time Braden corrected him.

When Braden was forced to work with the new prep chef Donna before the sun came up. And then witnessed her senseless butchering of his quail recipe at The Odd Duck. He simply lost his shit. The last thing he wanted was a repeat of yesterday with another newbie, and his choice of language showed his frustration.

Not that he had never sworn a day in his life, but even he had to admit that his NY potty mouth was over the top for six in the morning. And then Priya had to walk in. She grew more and more beet red from each of those choice words he uttered. Braden found it hard to contain himself when she sported the horrified look on her face. He actually wanted to take the bite out of his words. And possibly taste the sweet essence from her neck once her accent gave him enough reason to think she was a quiet Southern belle. She was a picture of perfection, and he yearned to drink her in. And in both the literal and theoretical sense. But her look of horror alone made him chuckle enough to forget about his horrible day with the cameraman. And for that, he was grateful. How a human could make his dead heart forget such an atrocity was beyond him, though.

He had mainly hired her because of her perky breasts. The cute accent that made him smile during the interview was merely an added bonus. Her drawl proved a welcome change to the harsh tones of his sharp New York one. He never once imagined that this woman would have any talent. Not one person he hired had even a sliver regarding gourmet cooking. Most chefs coming fresh from school have little flare, and he figured he'd have to mold Priya into what he needed her to be. But the spit-fire that came from her lips about food and professionalism told him otherwise. And that passion within her made him tongue-tied as he led her to his office.

That passion made his dick hard, and all he could think about was the heat they'd make in the kitchen, so he started showing her the recipes. When they reached for the note on the prosciutto, he felt an electric current shoot through his arm and right down to his core, making his dick strain at the zipper on his pants. If just a graze of her touch made him worry that his cock would pierce through his pants, he couldn't imagine what kissing her would feel like, or better yet, what having her pussy anchored around his shaft would be like. He hadn't experienced an ounce of attraction to a woman in probably a century, maybe two. Sure, he'd had his way with women because even a vampire has itches that needed a scratch. But those women meant nothing to him, probably because they were after his money and fame. It wasn't hard to read the minds of humans. Priya, however, wasn't after any of that. In fact, her primary goal was to see him succeed. It was something he never thought a human would do. All the ones he met were as selfish as vampires, only caring about and looking out for themselves. Her thoughts only intrigued him—even excited him, making him wonder if he had made a mistake hiring her. Because what if he got close to her? Every woman he had in his bed before filled his need. Priya was different, and he understood that the more he talked to her. She seemed to fill a hunger within him he assumed had died long ago.

Don't shit where you eat, Braden! You know that!

He now had to be careful around her because just the sight of her made him want so much more from her than she might be willing to give.

She's mine! I want her as my mate! No one else shall have her! No one!

Braden always lived his vampiric life simply. Whatever he wanted, he took, and to hell with the consequences—not that any mortal could refuse him, but he yearned for more from Priya. He wanted her to want him. And that was a dangerous thought. He had to get away from her and clear his head. Her breezy-smelling perfume, perfectly curvy body, and large breasts proved too much of an enormous distraction. Before Braden did the unthinkable, he needed to run out of there, claiming her lips and worshiping her body for the goddess she was. Acting upon his very desire for her right there in his kitchen. He needed to be inside her, to fuck her until she screamed his name. And to hell with the health codes, they'd be violating. He didn't give a shit about any of it. That was another red flag for him. Even when he cared for a woman, he never let them into his world. He kept his passion for cooking and his love for the show all to himself. No one could see that world, not after Celeste.

Thankfully, they still needed to finish up some voiceovers for his show. Braden hadn't planned on working on them until after The Odd Duck closed for the evening. The staff needed him at the restaurant, and he needed to spend time with them and Priya. Braden needed them prepped for the week's specials, if nothing else. He also wanted to observe Priya's management style while she interacted with his staff. Brayden hadn't realized it until Priya pointed it out—he'd been yelling and swearing at them an awful lot, especially these past couple of weeks. Braden did it out of stress because the show was all-consuming, and he knew he needed a sous-chef in his absence—hence hiring Priya.

He watched, mystified, as she artfully caressed the quail and rubbed the spiced mixture he gave her onto the breast. Fantasies of her stroking his chest with those same skillful hands washed over him. A picture of her wrapping her hand around his dick rushed over him, too. He quickly reached for the dutch oven and turned on his heel to pop it in the oven, thankful for having something else besides Priya to *do* in the most proverbial of senses. The idea of taping the voiceovers entered his mind again, and he deemed it the perfect excuse to leave her while he still could. Before her perfume tempted him even further, he barked a few orders for her to plate the food on her own, and then he turned on his heel and left the restaurant.

Don't look back! You'll never leave if you do!

It surprised him that his head overruled his conviction to stay as he hopped in his Mercedes-Maybach S-Class and drove towards the studio.

TIME SPENT AT THE STUDIO GREW LONG AND tedious, not because yesterday was a disaster but because Braden found it hard to keep Priya out of his mind. He finished wrapping up the few voiceovers they needed to tie up the show. And then found himself back at the restaurant as the lunch rush was about to get into full swing. He hoped he could control his urges, but she threw all hope out the window when he walked in and saw Priya teaching Donna how to make the quail dish.

Seeing the two of them cook in sync with each other made his heart pump with something foreign to him. The cavity that contained his dead heart seemed to compress—was that the human equivalent of joy? He couldn't be sure. After all, he was a pureblood vampire and had never known what it was like to have human experiences. He observed them further, and then his chest cavity swelled. Was that the human's version of pride soaring through his body? Priya clearly had the skill set he craved for this restaurant. He would have known that sooner if he had paid attention to something other than her chest during the interviewing process. Now a pang of guilt fluttered in his belly.

What kind of spell does this female hold over me?

He was becoming increasingly human as the experiences flooded him, and he wasn't sure if he liked what was happening.

"Thanks for setting Donna straight, Priya."

The attempt to compliment Priya came out weak, and he knew it. What was worse? He was still undermining Donna's abilities, which didn't sit well with his churning stomach. He fumbled far too much in this unfamiliar territory of humanity. It was as if every experience Priya threw his way was slicing through him like a Santoku knife. He'd hired perfection, and his need to tell her this grew within his core. Why was everything in his world suddenly so uncertain? Sadly, the only certainty in his rapidly changing world was him spinning on an opposite axis than everyone else. For the first time in his existence, he hated that he was a vampire, different from the humans around him.

After the comment, Donna lowered her head and walked away from him. Even though he understood she was merely responding to his stupid comment, he still couldn't help asking Priya what he did wrong. But why should Priya's mortal opinion of him matter this much?

"What's wrong with her? She's acting like I killed her cat."

It came out in a loud whisper because he really did know that answer, but he wasn't prepared for the disappointment she had for him. The frown that quickly replaced her smile tugged at his heart.

I wonder how many other women I have dismissed over the centuries? I really need to stop allowing my dick to do the talking! Wait? Why do I suddenly care? I'm a vampire! I shouldn't have a need to be seeking her approval!

He shook his head at the realization. He would never have thought about a woman's feelings before. But Priya was different. He needed, no—86 that! He *wanted* to be a better man for her, to please her in all ways possible, but then the barrage came quickly.

"Braden, do you not remember your tone and the foul language you used with her?"

Braden's eyes widened slightly, and he wasn't prepared for the disappointment in her tone.

"Oh, for Christ's sake! I swear all the time. That's just who I am."

The retort was all he could muster to put a wall up between them. The pain, guilt, and shame that now welled inside him were too much to bear.

"It's an unbecoming tone for an employer."

He witnessed Priya's frown again. It pulled at his heart in a direction he never thought possible. Could a human heart sink this low? It perplexed him that an organ could do such a thing in a human's body. And even though he was angry at himself for his unacceptable behavior, his mouth lashed out at the one and only person in front of him. She--and only she was the one and only person he never wanted to hurt.

"Oh, please, is Little Miss Prissy Priya going to tell me the error of my ways?"

He chuckled at his clever insult, hoping it would raise that wall between them even higher. But all it did was make his dead heart sink right down to his stomach. He tried to breathe, a silly notion for the undead since they didn't need to do something so human. But he felt stifled when he tried to grasp the oxygen in the room. It was as if his chest had a thousand bricks on it. Was Priya knocking down his wall? Another breath proved the answer true.

Priya winced. That made his knees buckle, and his stomach dropped right along with his heart. Then her face and ears turned beet red, indicating he had gone too far.

"For your information, my daddy was a preacher,

and he taught us we didn't need to swear to get our point across to others. He also taught us not to name-call. You do realize that name-calling is a form of bullying, and you, sir, are acting like a child with all your elementary school comments."

There was now no denying it. He pissed her off, and there was nothing he could do to take the words back.

She let out a breath of disgust and crossed her arms, preventing him access to her perfect chest.

"You know, I really thought I was getting through to you earlier when we were cooking the quail together. I guess I was wrong. It's like you've got a Jekyll and Hyde syndrome going on or something."

He didn't know whether he wanted to hug her or kiss her, but either way, he was right now at a loss for words. The woman was his match in wit, making her sexy as hell, and his dick twitched at the thought.

"Wow! I didn't think I hired a true Southern belle. This is going to be interesting. Very interesting, indeed."

The last sentence was for his own benefit rather than for her, but she didn't know that. He started walking towards his office, hoping to hide his clearly pronounced hard-on that was straining through the zipper of his pants.

This woman is driving me crazy!

He sat down in his chair and opened his laptop to start on next week's staff schedule. He hoped the distraction was enough to tame his little soldier down quickly. The last thing he wanted to do was take care of business if she barged into his office to give him another tongue lashing.

Shit! Stop. Thinking. About. Her. Tongue!

His gaze dropped to his dick and pleaded with it.

Dude! We don't have time for this little man. We are in the restaurant, so just quit it!

He tried to will it down, but that did little to nothing to ease the ache raging through his core. His door burst open.

See, little man!

His eyes locked onto the intrusion. It surprised him that it took Priya this long to barge in, but then again, it was dinner rush.

"You need to understand that I am a true Southern belle, and because I am a lady, I demand that you curb your curse words while you are around me. I also expect to be treated like a lady. If you speak to me, your eyes better be locked onto mine. That's the northern position further up from my chest! When you hired me, I was under the impression that this was a professional kitchen, so I expected nothing but professional behavior coming from you. If you can't meet these terms, I will quit. Do I make myself clear?"

Her voice was shaky, and her chest was heaving as a fiery red replaced her porcelain complexion. Her nostrils flared with each word she spat out when her gaze locked onto him.

Once done, she crossed her arms and breathed in and out through her mouth three long, deliberate times. She was sexy as hell when she was angry at him, and all Braden wanted to do was kiss her as a reward for that gorgeous display of passion.

"Well? Am I making myself clear?" She huffed the words out.

Braden blinked a couple of times before responding. He understood he needed to apologize to her and work on being a better man. She desired that, and he wanted more than anything, including his own passions, to give that to her.

"I'm sorry, Ms. Priya. I will ensure that I don't swear around you as much as I did today. It pains me that I've made you uncomfortable. From now on, I will be the perfect gentleman around you. I hope you can forgive me." He tried not to make the words sound trite, but they were pretty foreign as they were fumbling around in his mouth. He hadn't apologized to a vampire in a century, and as for a human, it was far longer than that. The last time was Celeste.

Priya blinked twice and let out a long breath.

"I suppose I can forgive you if you promise to curb it." She said with a half-smile.

Braden looked up at the wall clock in his office.

"Well, the dinner rush should end soon. Please see to everything running smoothly. You've been here almost as long as I have today, so once the rush is over —how about I take you out for a welcome to the team drink?"

Priya's eyes widened.

"Ah? A drink?"

31

"Yes. A welcome to the team drink. I do this with all of my management staff."

"Ah." Her cheeks turned beet red again.

"Don't tell me—not only did your father teach you not to swear—but he also taught you that drinking a glass of wine isn't a Christian thing to do either? I thought only the Puritans and the Mormons practiced abstinence from alcohol. I mean—didn't Jesus turn water into wine and all?" He spouted out quickly, desperate to get her to come with him.

Of course, it was all a lie. Brayden took no other employee out for a drink before.

"Jesus did, yes. And I drink alcohol. That's not the issue."

"So, what's the issue?" His eyes were trying to search her for an answer.

"I don't date people I work with."

Her eyes looked at the floor. She tried to conceal it, but her face blushed yet again.

"It's just a drink." He said as he stood up from his desk and moved close to her. He raised her head with his index finger to make her meet his gaze. "No need to get your panties in a bunch about this. Besides, if I were to ask you out, I'd be taking you to dinner."

"Okay. I guess that would be okay then—but just a drink."

"Great! I'm driving, though."

"Can't I just follow you?" She asked with widened eyes.

"No need to do that. In fact, I insist on driving us there, and I'll drive you back here once we are done."

"Well, I guess that will be okay. Let me tend to the dinner rush, and I guess I'll see you in a few."

Braden nodded and then grabbed some papers off of his desk. The scheduling was already done for the restaurant. And twice over, but he needed to focus on something to keep his mind from racing.

There was no denying that he liked her and wanted to take her out on a date, but he was a vampire who had no business dating a mortal. He looked at the wall clock and had a full hour to wait for the dinner rush to be over. As he let out a sigh, he poured his eyes over the scheduling again. After a few cuts, he looked at the wall clock again and was surprised that it was almost eight pm. He pinned the schedule on the board outside his office, headed towards the kitchen to meet up with Priya, and found her wiping down the prep counter.

"All set, Priya?"

"Yup. Let me just get my purse."

Chapter Three

REALITY BITES

P riya slipped into the buttery diamond white leather seat on the passenger's side of Braden's Nautical Blue Mercedes-Maybach S-Class. She caressed the soft leather around either side of her thighs. The curve of the bucket seat hugged her back perfectly, making her instantly relax in the seat's comfort. She felt the day's tension melt into the leather and let out a soft hum of pleasure.

Braden slid into the driver's side with a smile.

"Now, do you get why I wanted to drive?"

"Definitely. It's a very nice car. It's been a long while since I've been in one of these. I owned one—well, I owned an E 450 Coup in Moonlight White Metallic and Macchiato Beige and Magma Grey leather. I really miss my boy." Priya said as her hands explored more of the interior.

"Oh? What happened?"

"I got one new, and I crashed and totaled it. The

accident wasn't my fault, but since I only had a job washing dishes—at least at the time—I couldn't afford to replace it. Maybe now that I'm in management, I can think about owning a pre-owned, but I might go for something totally different. I've always wanted to drive with a stick."

"Well, I'm sorry to hear about your accident. How long ago did that happen?"

"About three years ago. I'm finally fully recovered from it, too. I had to get some back surgery done, and that was a bitch."

"I can imagine. I'm sorry it took so long for you to mend." Braden pressed his lips together before placing the car in drive.

"Yeah, but I'm better now."

"So, if you want to learn how to drive a stick, what kind of car would you go for?"

"A Jag."

Braden chuckled.

"I've never met a woman who could drive a stick."

"Hey—don't judge! I'm great with the clutch! I never stalled it out once when an ex tried to teach me. My only problem is that I couldn't figure out the damned gear changes to save my life. The whole hand-eye coordination threw me off."

Priya's mouth went dry as thoughts of Jordan rushed to the surface of her mind.

Braden belted out a full laugh.

"The clutch is the hardest part! How can you manage that and not be able to handle the gear shifts?"

"It's just part of my charm. I can easily maneuver the hardest of tasks, but I have the biggest problems with the simple stuff. Don't even get started with simple math equations."

"Oh? So, you are more into calculus and or quantum physics. I take it?"

Priya laughed.

"Something like that."

Braden pulled into a parking space at The Roosevelt Room about 25 minutes into the light conversation in the car. He hadn't even noticed how long they'd been in the car because their conversation flowed at incredible ease.

"This place looks interesting. I've never been—but then again—I haven't been to many places because I recently moved to this area. I was born and raised here in Round Rock, Texas, but my move to Austin is recent—within the past three years."

"I've come here a couple of times. One of my dear friends owns the place."

"Really? That's cool! How long have you known your friend?" Priya asked.

"Oh, we go back quite a way," Braden said as he shoved his hands in his pockets after opening the passenger side door for Priya.

"So, grade school?"

"Yeah. Something like that." Braden broke his gaze from her and darted his eyes to the pavement.

He was never one to lie to any vampire. His integrity kept him on the up and up. And the strange part? He never lied to a human, either. Granted—the only interaction he had with humans had been food-related—them either preparing it for the customers or serving it. Sure, occasionally, he'd drink from a human. He was a pureblood, so it wasn't necessary. He didn't crave blood like someone who was turned by a half-blood vampire. Dracula, or Drake, as many of the ones sired by him called him, was the one that he called his master. But not because Drake bit him. No. Drake fell in love with a mortal who was Braden's mother. The fling was short-lived because Drake went back to Lilith, his first love, and Braden grew up without knowing his father or his powers until he became an adult five months after his birth. Sadly, his mother did not survive giving birth to him, and he was raised by his aunt. Once he became a full-fledged adult, he asked his aunt if she wanted to become immortal. She declined, and that's when Braden realized how precious yet fleeting life was for mortals. It was then that he chose never to drink from a human. He'd survive on food and beverages—like the humans, apparently, just like his father.

But Priya? She tempted him. Her blood was far more intoxicating than any other human's. Most had a metallic scent, tainted by many things they'd done to abuse their body. Gone were the days of a human smelling and tasting like a fine wine. And that was the only thing keeping him from drinking another human until now.

This was all unfamiliar territory for him, and he

wasn't sure why any of it mattered. Sure, humans couldn't know of his existence, so he always kept to himself. And he shied away from a serious relationship with a woman—just to avoid the temptation should one arise. And yet, something within him wanted him to bare his soul to Priya. Still, he hired her as an employee, which would help him make an insane amount of money, and that was the purpose of her being here—nothing more. At least, it shouldn't be anything more.

The thing was, he was seriously rethinking his views on humankind now that she entered his life. He'd been around for centuries and fucked every woman he found attractive simply because he could.

She was different and was what he had been searching for throughout his existence. The only problem was that she had made it clear that she wasn't looking for anything with him since he was her boss. A pang touched his heart as he thought about her apprehension of this drink date.

"So, should we head on in?" She asked with a smile as the bouncer opened the rope for them to enter.

"Yes, let's."

Chapter Four
LIQUID COURAGE

He extended his arm out to escort her inside. She wrapped her arms around one of his biceps as if she had been doing it naturally for years. The touch electrified her in ways she'd never assumed possible. How could a man have this much of an effect on her? It wasn't like this was her first rodeo. She'd been with many successful men before—heck, she even almost married one! His eyes met hers, and she briefly smiled before looking away. She found it hard to resist the temptation glistening in his dark irises. Her core instantly set ablaze with desire. Oh, how she wanted something more. But he was her boss, and she had to remember not to cross that line. Crossing such a line would only end in heartache for her.

It had been three long years since she was with a man. And it had been three years since she ever trusted one with her heart. Since then, she kept men at arm's length. To grow attached to someone who would hurt her made no sense in her life anymore—not after Jordan. And she'd be damned if she trotted down the same path with Braden, who seemed to exude everything she was trying to avoid.

This man swore while working; he attended all the exclusive celebrity parties and seemed to be photographed with a new woman in every trash rag. All the tabloids made him out to be a bad boy who only cared about his own gratifications. These things she'd already had with Jordan, and she had enough of the limelight with *the* Jordan Price.

That man took her heart, her money, and all of her dignity. The last thing she needed was an arrogant, selfish 2.0 version of the same type of man in her life. She did not intend to fall for the gorgeous god who wasn't taking his eyes off her as they entered the establishment. It seemed odd to her for him to do that. She'd figured the pretty boy would have sported his roving eyes at this point in the evening. And yet, he wasn't. His eyes were soft, inviting, and intermixed was something behind them, making her want to trust him.

Daddy always said honesty would be in the eyes of the man talking to you.

She never gave the advice much thought when it came to Jordan because she was truly blind by her love for him. She refused to see the dishonesty in his, which probably should have been her first red flag. It wasn't until they were carting Jordan off to jail for all of his crimes that she finally saw the deceit surrounding her.

They found him guilty of so many embezzlement charges that Jordan will be lucky if he ever sees the light of day again. And no matter how sad it sounded to Priya three years ago, she now finds there is an emptiness in place of her compassion for him. A void that has been the driving force of avoiding any man who even looked in her general direction. She never wanted to be duped again. It's one thing to be cheated upon, and she'd have that happen to her before, but when a man embezzles away every cent you've ever earned on your own, it does something to you. Only this kind of betrayal runs deeper than any other. At least, it's what she had always thought.

"So, I know I should have asked you this in the interview, but honestly, your resume impressed me so much that I talked about other things while you were there. What got you started in a career of cooking?"

Priya's eyes widen at his question. She had been prepared to give him some type of bullshit answer during the interview and frankly be done with her intimacy on the matter. But now, she had to provide him with something at least a little truthful. If she didn't, she'd find it hard to keep up a lie now that she was working for him. She hadn't lied to anyone a day in her life, and she didn't want to start now. But how could she tell him that the only reason she got into a cooking career was that her ex, Jordan, never thought she could do it? No, she had to make the truth work for her. And hopefully, Braden wouldn't bombard her with questions about her jerk of an ex.

"Honestly? Someone hurt me three years ago, and I had to start my life over because of it. My ex was awful, and the only thing that kept me sane through all of it was cooking. There's just something about creating a meal from scratch which gave me the power over something. I needed that desperately in my life. Of course, pounding the heck out of a cutlet helped a lot, too—not gonna lie. I thought making a career out of it would continue to keep me sane. My daddy always taught me that life is filled with many insane moments, and they shape us into the people we are today. I get what he meant, but I need comfort when surrounded by chaos. Food does that for me."

Braden lowered his gaze to her lips before meeting her eyes again.

"I'm sorry to hear that someone hurt you so deeply. I would never do that to someone as beautiful as you are on the inside and out." His eyes widened, and his gaze fell to the floor the minute the words escaped his mouth. "I mean—I—um, I'm sorry. I shouldn't be saying things like that because you made it clear to me earlier—" His voice trailed, and he swallowed hard.

She found her hand palming his before they made a retreat from the bartop they were now sitting at.

"It's okay." She said after she put down her now empty glass of wine.

She didn't realize she guzzled the drink within the

first few minutes of them talking after the server had put it down on the table. She was glad to tell someone the truth about *the* Jordan Price without falling apart. Usually, she always did. Part of that was guilt because many of daddy's parishioners bought into Jordan, just like she did. And that killed her because many of them spent their retirement funds on his Ponzi scheme. After all, the ass sold it like it was the investment of a lifetime. Even Priya trusted her life savings with this man she would marry. It turned out Jordan was a liar and cheat far worse than one who bedded another woman. She could have held her head high in their hometown if he'd done that to her. Sure everyone in town didn't blame her. They were Christian and God-fearing people. But she couldn't face any of them—not until she made enough on her own to pay each one of them back! Braden's kind eyes made bearing her soul to him easier. She'd probably never tell him the entire story, but right now, as he squeezed her hand, she'd felt something she hadn't in what seemed like forever. She felt worthy of being in someone else's presence. He gave her a half smile as his eyes glistened in the dimmed lighting of the bar. He appeared grateful for her understanding of his apparent blunder with words, but there also appeared to be confusion in his eyes. At first, Priya didn't care because she could explain away anything she'd just said to him and with a confidence she hadn't had with herself in what seemed like a lifetime.

"But is it? Priya, you said yourself that you don't

do friendships outside of work. And frankly, I was the same way before I met you."

She saw his Adam's apple move distinctively, signifying he'd swallowed hard. He then took a sip of the red wine that the bartender had placed in front of him. Was he feeling the same things she was? His gaze went from her to the empty glass. He motioned to the server to get her another one. She wanted to protest because she told him only one drink, but they'd just gotten here, and she was actually having fun. Of course, she wasn't sure if that was the Pinot Grigio she'd guzzled doing the talking.

She watched his gaze lock onto her once more, lowering it to her lips once more. She found her body inching closer to his. It was acting on instinct—or probably the wine—definitely the wine!

Crap!

"Maybe I was wrong about saying that?" She said as she leaned forward. Her lips were mere inches from his, and her fingers were now caressing his arm from his wrist up to his shoulder.

Why am I doing this? I've never gotten buzzed off of one drink!

He shut his eyes and sucked in a breath. When he opened them again, Priya saw his irises turn red. She lowered her gaze to screw her eyes shut and discreetly shook her head. There was no way he had red eyes, so she was seeing things now. She'd never been roofied, but Braden wouldn't do that to her. She was his employee! Or would he?

"Priya, don't do this. Please. I'm not willing to sleep with you tonight."

What?

Why would he say something like that? Unless she really was drunk!

Crap again!

Priya sucked in a breath. She tried to look away from him before her eyes revealed the horror of his words. She never expected him to reject her because he had been making advances on her all day and all night. But clearly, he was! The thought terrified her and gave her *the warm fuzzies* all at once.

I must save face! Stupid alcohol! I knew I shouldn't have gone out with him! I haven't had a glass of wine since Jordan went to jail.

She retreated completely towards her side of the table. She guzzled half of her fresh glass of Pinot Grigio in a single sip. That was a definite mistake, but she couldn't help it now because she hoped the liquid would give her an ounce of courage to get her out of the mess she'd just stepped into. As she put down her glass, he grasped her wrist.

"You are misreading what I meant. Please let me explain before you dismiss me as an ass." He shut his eyes and took in a breath before opening them once more. As he locked onto her gaze again, he continued with his thoughts effortlessly, and Priya was in awe of the confidence he exuded. "I'm sorry. I promised to do better with the swearing, and I still need to work on it. But that's not what I mean to say to you right now. I want you to know that I like you, Priya. I like you a lot. But I'll be damned if I'm going to let that wine we drink do the talking tonight."

Her eyes widened. Shock riddled her face, and she knew it. Was he accusing her of drinking too much? Clearly, she was! But that's only because she hadn't been on a date in what seemed like a lifetime.

"What are you saying, then?" The words escaped her before she even gave them permission.

"I like you, Priya. And the more time I spend with you, the more I don't want to play games. Life is just too short to do that. I want to date you, and I don't want just one night with you. Call me selfish to want more from you if that is what you wish, but that's the truth."

Priya's gaze lowered slightly to her wineglass. She grabbed his hand and made circular motions in his palm as she talked. It was a stupid gesture, and she hadn't even realized she'd done it till now.

"I don't want to have a one-night-stand with you either, Braden. It's just—" Her voice trailed, and at this point, she didn't know why, exactly.

He was saying what she wanted to hear from him. But?

He's a player, Priya. Never forget that.

He cupped her cheek with one hand and raised her chin with his index finger of his other to meet his gaze.

"Someone's hurt you. I get that. I have been, too. Let me try to fix a little of your hurt. Please?"

"Braden, I can't do this. I can't. I mixed business

and pleasure before, and it was a huge mistake. He hurt me in ways I don't think I'll ever recover from."

Braden looked into her eyes as if he was bearing witness to all the heartache Jordan had put her through.

"Breathe. Please? Breathe in and out for me for one minute. You look like you will have a panic attack, and I refuse for that to happen on a date." His gaze was methodical and full of worry.

"So now you admit that this is a date?" She smiled slightly while breathing in through her nose and out through her mouth, a little more pronounced than before. "Who knew that my falling apart in front of you would be the key to you admitting your attraction to me?"

"Priya, I think we've established that I like you. A lot. And yes, that had a little to do with hiring you. I'll admit that. But I never want you to think that I think of you any less because of that attraction. You are so talented, Priya. I'm amazed at how far you have come in only a few years in this field. Your passion has taken you to great places so far. I can only imagine where else you will go. I'd love to be around to witness your ride to fame." He half-smiles at her as he continues to caress her cheek.

She lowers her head slightly.

"I'm not the type of person who deserves praise like that. Not after what my ex did to me and everyone that believed in me in my hometown." She frowned.

Tears formed in the corner of her eyes, and she desperately tried to blink them back.

His eyes widened only slightly.

"Now I know why you looked so familiar to me. You used to be Jordan Price's girl, right?"

She now couldn't hold back the tears. They were full flowing and staining her cheeks as they rolled down her face. She tried to wipe as many as she could away before responding.

"Yes, yes, I was. And it is a time in my life that I really would rather forget."

"I understand. But," Braden said as he cupped her face in both hands and wiped the remaining tears with his thumbs. "I'm not him, and all I want is for you to be happy and feel safe. You deserve that."

His lips were just a breath from her ear.

"I really want to kiss you, Priya. Can I?"

She bit her lip, causing his eyes to darken with desire, and before she knew it, his lips were crashing on hers.

The kiss was inviting and seductive all at once, making her melt into him. As he sucked on her bottom lip, her panties soaked, and it wouldn't be long before she asked him to come home with her. She wasn't sure if it was the wine or the fact that she hadn't been with a man in forever that made her lose all of her inhibitions. But she had to resist him because that kiss awakened something she thought had been long gone within her. He wrapped his arm around her waist and pulled her closer to him—his cock thickening against her outer thigh with each entanglement of their tongues. He moaned softly before pulling his lips away and resting his forehead on hers.

"I need to stop before I ask you to come home with me." He said as he took a swig of the remaining wine in his glass and motioned for the server to return.

"May I have the check, please?" He asked before returning his gaze back to Priya. "More than anything, I would love to wake up with you by my side, but? And I can't believe I'm saying this—I should take you back to your car."

"Yeah, okay."

She gave him a smile she really wasn't feeling. He was right—hell, even she was thinking it! So why did she feel as if someone just sucker punched her? The rejection seemed to linger like a dark cloud, chilling her shoulders down to her bones.

He cupped her cheek as he handed the server his credit card. The gesture was sweet, and his hand sent heat to her face, but she couldn't help but wonder if he was only doing it to let her down easy. Clearly, Braden doesn't sleep with every woman that crosses his path. He was selective because he had no intention of sleeping with her.

"It's been a long time since I've been looking forward to getting to work. And I have you to thank for that." He smiled at her as he guided her out to the car.

Chapter Five
ROCK STAR

Her crying pained him so much that he was willing to do anything to release the anguish clouding over her face. In all his years as a vampire, he never once desired to take the pain away from someone. His powers seemed to fix every problem he encountered, except this one. And for the first time in his existence, he felt utterly powerless.

Still, he had to convince her she was beautiful and worthy of love, especially after finding out who had hurt her. He may be a monster and undeserving of her love, but the asshole who hurt her didn't deserve a shred of her beauty.

Her tears were free-flowing now, and Braden grew desperate to cleanse her of the affliction known as Jordan Price. Flicking as many tears away as he could with his thumbs, he tried the only other thing powerful enough to make her see the beauty radiating within her. He kissed her, deep and long.

An awakening grew within him and shot straight to his groin. It had been a few years since he had experienced anything remotely close to this feeling before now. And he didn't want this night with her to end. Not when she was guzzling her drinks and relaxing with him. Sure, he found many women attractive, and they helped to scratch an itch, but this? He knew what this was, and the desire bubbling within him made his dick pulsate through his pants. He was aching to be inside her, pleasing her, filling her with as much exhilaration as she could handle. And then taking her further until she was screaming his name.

Celeste was someone he thought loved him, and she was also someone he'd chosen to exist with. He even told her his secret of being a vampire—something he'd never shared with any other human before. And not because he was scared for his life. He was not even fearing exposure of his kind to the mortals. No. He never shared his secret out of fear of acceptance. What human would willfully bed a vampire? A monster that a human should revolt at the sight of. Still, she accepted him for who he was—or so he thought.

As the months of prep for the cooking show started, gatherings in the Hollywood limelight occurred. Braden invited Celeste to as many as he could, but she grew angered that he didn't ask her to them all. When he overheard her talking to the tabloids about his life off-camera, that was the last straw that broke the proverbial camel's back. He knew very few people would believe that he was a vampire. Humans enjoyed the legends, but most still had a silly notion that vampires were merely human psychics who fed off of another mortal's energy—not their blood. It still didn't stop her from trying to profit from his—as the tabloids put it, "self-proclaimed vampirism," and he then realized that she was more of a monster than even he could ever be.

Without hesitation, he erased her memory of him, brought her back to her old apartment, and left. After that, he closed off his heart, vowing to never do this to himself again by loving another human. He kept that promise to himself for many years until he met Priya.

With her, everything became different. Priya wanted nothing more than to see him succeed. He knew this when he read her mind during the interview. But now, sitting beside her, he couldn't violate her mind. Even if he did, he knew she loathed the limelight he was in. She said it in not so many words. Her face gave it away once he'd uttered the name of the person who hurt her. He wished he could take it back—and he could! His power to erase a human's mind was right at his fingertips. But something tugged at his dead heart. He didn't want to defile her memories of this evening. If he made her forget each scorching touch, each shaky breath she made when she brushed her fingers over his body, it may kill him. He would rather die a thousand mortal deaths than defile her in such an intimate way. Southern belles are pure by sheer nature. He knew that, and that's why he didn't want to taint her beauty. He just hoped she would overlook his monstrous side if he ever weakened to the point of telling her. But something deep within him that shook him to his core told him not to tell her of his nightmarish side. And not because he was afraid to. No. Something told him she'd accept him for what he was. He just didn't want to bestow such a burden on her.

The next day came too early, and he had showered and dressed for work before his alarm went off. Today would be different, which made him smile.

He drove to the restaurant and pulled in at the same time Priya did. He met her at her car and opened up the driver's side, and she smiled as she got out of the vehicle.

"Hi."

"Hi."

They both walked up to the entrance, not saying much else to one another. After shutting off the alarm in the restaurant, Braden opened the door for Priya to come in.

"I'll have a key and code ready for you by early next week. For now, you can come in with the rest of the crew if you so choose. No one but me needs to be here at 7 am."

"If it's alright with you, I'd rather get here early so I can prep the specials. That's kind of my thing."

Braden smiled.

"That's always been my thing, too."

"Well, I'd better get to work. I don't want the boss saying I'm a slacker on my second day." She said with a chuckle before pressing her hand over her mouth. "Oh, dear! I'm sorry! The hostess told me yesterday that you hate being called the boss. I didn't mean to offend you."

It was true. Braden always hated that because teasing would always ensue about the show after that. But she didn't mean it that way, making the jest less like a knife wedging into his back.

"Yeah, I'd better get the bar inventory done." He turned on his heel, headed to the bar with a clipboard, and tried to focus on the task. Still, he found himself looking over at the kitchen every few minutes just to get a glimpse of her walking by the windows on the doors.

After about an hour of counting bottles, he was finally done and headed back to the kitchen. He opened the door and found Priya passionately pouring her heart over the citrus salmon dish they decided on as the special for the day, and he smiled.

"Oh, good, you're back! What do you think?" She asked as she dipped a spoon into the sauce mixture and lifted it to his lips.

He blew on the spoon slightly and watched her eyes heat at the gesture. The hooded look made him want her, but since they were in the kitchen, all he could do was tease her, which turned him on so much so that his dick twitched. He slowly opened his mouth to take in the sauce and made sure his lips consumed the spoon in its entirety. And well before, he slowly and deliberately took the full hilt of the flavor she was offering—the burst of flavors mixed in his mouth. He almost came in his underwear from not only the explosion playing with the back of his tongue. But also from her hooded gaze.

"I'm guessing that I nailed it, Braden?"

Oh, honey! I love the way you are saying my name, and I love how you say the word nailed!

"Honey, my mouth had an orgasm, so yes, you nailed it."

"I'm glad my food does wonderful things to you."

He didn't think it was humanly possible, but her eyes darkened even more, and then she licked her lips. Heat rushed right to his dick, his pants tightened, his cock so fully erected that he almost couldn't breathe. He had to taste her lips, but he wouldn't do that in the kitchen, so he wrapped his arm around her waist and guided her through the door leading to the restaurant's back alley. He pressed her body against the cool brick wall and nibbled on her ear.

"That food makes me want to express my gratitude to the chef personally. So? Exactly how should I thank her?" His voice was a low growl as he whispered over the lobe. "I appreciate such delicacy, and I need to express just how much that dish is rocking my world."

He pinned her wrists against the building and trailed kisses down her cheek. His mouth claimed hers, and she let out a soft moan before he trailed kisses down her neck and onto her collarbone.

"And I can't seem to get enough of it. It's simply mouth-watering." His lips grazed over the fabric of her shirt until he reached for each of her nipples, and he sucked over the material until they peaked with desire for him.

"Hmm. Braden, as much as I like your appreciation, we really have to get back inside. The rest of the employees will be here any minute, and I'm sure the last thing you want is for them to see you like this with me."

Braden released his grip on Priya's wrists and pulled back to search her eyes.

"What makes you assume I would keep my affection for you a secret from them? Because," His voice trailed slightly as he closed his eyes and sucked in a deep breath before continuing, "I'm not like that asshole ex of yours. I would never hide you from my world. I want to share it with you, Priya."

She splayed her hands on his chest.

"No, I didn't mean it like that. I just meant that I will understand if you want to keep this from the employees, professionally speaking. Because I get it."

He palmed her cheek.

"Clearly, you don't get it because I meant it when I told you last night that I wanted to date you. And when I date someone, I don't keep them a secret from everyone else."

"Braden, I understand—at least now I do. But you

have a reputation to think about. You are a rockstar. And I'm pretty sure your publicist will not be too happy with me. Because you dating someone whose ex was so bad that he not only embezzled from the seniors in my hometown? But also did it with every charity organization I was involved with. I don't want my past to hurt you! It would be bad enough when the press finds out that I work here—and I am not looking forward to that day because it would kill me if I destroyed your career! Maybe I should just quit, so I don't hurt you like that."

"Priya, stop! I will not have you talking about us as if we broke up before we even get to date number two."

"I know. It's just—well? I don't even know. This is all so confusing, and I don't want you getting hurt just because I like you. I can't be selfish about this. I have to think about you and your well-being. That's why I'm committing so much verbal diarrhea right now." She huffed out a large and heaving puff of air after she barraged him with these words.

"How about you let me worry about myself? Okay? And as far as this goes," He said as he waved a hand between them, "let's keep this out of the press until we are both comfortable enough to label what we feel for each other. Fair enough?"

"Fair enough."

He pulled her into his arms once more, wanting to breathe in her woodsy perfume before heading back into the restaurant.

"Come get a drink with me again tonight after work, please?"

She pulled back from him slightly and gazed into his eyes before responding.

"I'd like that."

Chapter Six
ONCE BITTEN

I t was another morning of complete bliss. They had spent almost every waking moment together since their drink date earlier in the month. She found it hard to keep her hands off him, especially when they would steal moments with each other in the back alley after the dinner rush. And with each kiss he gave her, she fell more and more in love with him.

The romance may not have been long, but he understood her and what she needed out of life. He was nothing like any of the men she had ever dated before, and she had dated enough to know that Braden was different. His lifestyle to everyone else reading the tabloids may seem like he's a bad boy whose heart is only dedicated to self-gratification and one-night stands. But the real Braden Boss was nothing like that at all. They hadn't slept together yet—something the tabloids might have thought impossible for the lady's man to do. But Braden wanted her to feel comfortable with trusting another person in her life again. He was so concerned with her feelings that he didn't play the games she was accustomed to in all her other relationships.

She rolled over to shut off her phone alarm that had just sounded and smiled. This week was the first time in her life that she woke up before the alarm instead of with it. Her life never seemed to have any purpose until now, and that purpose was making beautiful meals at The Odd Duck with Braden Boss.

She jumped out of bed and rushed out the door after showering, pulling on her chef's uniform, and brushing her teeth. Once through the front door of The Odd Duck, she was greeted by his smile that made her body awaken better than any caffeine ever could.

"Please come into my office so we can discuss the specials for this weekend, Ms. Priya." He said with a professional tone in front of Donna.

There was no longer any swearing from his lips. Just mutual respect Priya always knew he had for everyone. Now, it showed through both his actions and words.

His gait was quick and determined. Priya had to jog just to keep up with him. He closed the door behind her and locked it once she entered the room. His lips were a breath apart from hers as he pressed his body against hers. She felt his stiff cock pressing against her inner thigh.

"I had a hard time waiting to see you this morning, Priya." He said as he slid his arm around her waist to pull her to him to claim her lips. "I can't wait to spend the entire weekend with you. I wish we could start now." He whispered over her ear before sucking on the lobe.

She palmed his chest and then gently pushed him away.

"Braden, I can't wait either, but we need to get through today first, so what would you like to create for today's specials?"

Braden let out a guttural groan.

"This isn't fair. Woman, why must you insist on making an honest man out of me?"

"Because it is part of my job description to do so." She said with a smirk.

"As my sous chef or as my girlfriend?" He said with a matching smile.

"Girlfriend, huh? I must admit that I really like the sound of that, so I'll say both!" She chuckled.

"Okay. We can get back to business but on one condition! You leave with me after the lunch rush, and I take you for an early dinner. I can't wait 12 hours to be able to kiss you. That would be too tortuous."

"Deal. But only because Gary from the bar agreed to be the manager tonight."

He raised a brow.

"Did you ask him to be?"

"I may have since I was supposed to close."

"You sly devil!"

"I'm guessing it is you with the devilish undertones

since you enjoy pressing me up against walls so much." She said with another chuckle.

After they quickly decided on the smoked pork shoulder and the fried quail as the specials, she unlocked the door to the office and headed straight for the prep area to brief the other cooks.

Before Priya glanced at the clock, the lunch rush was over, and Braden was by her side.

"I've already told Gary that we are leaving. Shall we go?"

"Let me just get my purse, and then we can head out."

He led her to the car and drove her to the nearest Whole Foods Market. As Braden was pulling into a space, Priya gazed at him with a furrowed brow.

"Why are we stopping here?"

"I'm cooking for you at my place. If you want to go out for a drink after—we can—but I was hoping we'd stay in for the entire weekend." He said with a smile.

"That sounds nice, but if you want me over for the weekend, we will have to stop at my place so I can pick up some clothes. I only planned for a night."

"Well, for what I'm planning, you won't need any clothes, but I can head to your place on the way to mine. If you so chose to wear clothes—that is." He said with a wry smile.

He shut the passenger door for her and headed in. They quickly decided on a beef roast, some Brussels sprouts, and yellow potatoes for dinner. They stopped over at the wine section so Braden could pick up some red wine for his chateaubriand he'd be making for the evening.

While perusing the isle, he settled on a Bordeaux with a 2015 vintage and bought three.

"One for the dish and a couple for us to share over dinner and the weekend." He said with a smile.

AFTER THE PURCHASES AND GOING TO PRIYA'S place to pack a weekend bag, Braden made quick of the prep work for the dinner. He placed the chateaubriand in the oven to roast and grabbed a couple of glasses to pour two wine glasses of what was left of the bottle he used for cooking. He handed a glass to Priya and raised his.

"Here's to our budding relationship that grows into something more special with each passing moment."

Priya smiled and clinked her glass with his. Braden placed his glass down and pulled her into his arms. He pressed kisses to his cheek and jaw before trailing kisses down her neck. Desire rose deep within his belly. It was an experience he was so familiar with. He'd had desire before, but this seemed so much different. Braden knew he had to tell her he was a vampire, but he feared her reaction. Sure he can fight the urge to drink from her. He was a pureblood, after all. But that didn't mean that she'd have enough trust in him to refrain from sucking her dry. He'd already tried to tell her but chickened out at the last minute. And now that they would be with each other the entire weekend, he felt he should say it to her before they sat down for dinner. But her scent was so good, and he could only think about taking her clothes off.

"We've got some time to kill while the food is roasting." His lips trailed down to the exposed part of her chest. "I think I can find a way to keep us entertained while waiting for the timer to go off."

Her gaze darkened as she clasped her hands around his neck and her legs around his waist. He smiled, led her off to the bedroom, and laid her on the bed. He kissed each exposed part of her skin that revealed itself to him while he removed all of her clothing. He then removed all of his before straddling his legs over her thighs.

"You are so, so beautiful, Priya." He said as he slipped two fingers inside of her. She was already drenched, and that made his dick twitch with excitement. "I want to taste you."

She let out a soft moan and arched that perfect pussy of hers to give him better access, and that was all he needed. He circled her clit with his tongue and continued to nibble, tease, and suck until she was just at the edge of orgasm. He slipped three fingers inside her this time and bit her clit, sending her soaring over the edge as her sex clamped down around his fingers. He continued to suck and lick her until something just as pleasing as her vanilla butterscotch musky scent came to the forefront of his mouth. It was her blood. In his excitement, he bit too hard, and her delicious blood began to fill his tongue. He licked the hurt to seal the wound.

God, how could I have been so stupid? I can't do this to her. I can't hurt her like this!

He wanted to pull back and run from her before he hurt her any further. Not that she'd know because he already sealed her wound. But she kept a firm grip on his head as she played with his hair and guided his lips back to her sex.

"Please don't stop, baby. I need you."

He reached for her hands and placed them over her head.

"I need to be inside you. I need your pussy wrapped around my cock."

He wasn't lying because he did want to be inside her, but the thought of hurting her made his stomach churn. She arched her back, and his cock quickly slipped into her slick folds. She started to thrust, and that's when his dick took over, slamming deep inside her wet center over and over until both of their bodies were slick with sweat. A pool of pleasure surrounded them. He felt her orgasm peaking, and that was when he began to soar over the edge himself. He continued to thrust in, out, in, out, in, and out again until her quickening subsided.

"That was amazing. You're amazing." She said as he pulled himself up to meet her gaze.

"You're amazing too." He kissed her forehead before sitting up and searching for his clothes. He shucked on his shirt before continuing. "Why don't you take a shower, and I'll go check on dinner."

He was out the door before she could protest.

Stupid, stupid, stupid!

He let out a sigh as he turned on the oven light. At least one thing went right tonight. The meal was browning beautifully.

What am I going to do?

The idea hit him like a Mack Truck.

I should break up with her because she'd be safer without me in her life.

He let out a breath he didn't realize he was holding in.

Not now, though. After dinner. It should be after dinner, and then I'll drive Priya home because I can't trust myself around her.

She bolted into the kitchen. Her hair was plastered to her face.

"Did I do something wrong?"

"What do you mean, Priya?"

"I just figured you'd shower with me or cuddle after we? We?" Her voice trailed.

He wanted to tell her that he was freaking out. He even tried to tell her the truth about being a vampire, but in the end, he settled on being a coward to keep her safe.

"Priya, why would I cuddle? You know I'm a billionaire bad boy."

It was a dickish thing to say, and the words cut him as if he was filleting himself with a butcher knife. Her face transformed within seconds from a beautifully confident and loving woman to one that couldn't put the brick and mortar up fast enough between them.

"I see. I should go." She said as she pulled out her phone.

"I can drive you if you want."

"No, thank you. I don't want to put you out just because we had sex. I'll grab an Uber." She uttered the sex as if it was the vilest thing in the world, and maybe it was because the act they performed wasn't like that. Even when he drank from her, he was more intimate than he'd ever been with a woman. No. They made love, not sex. Bile filled his stomach and shot up his throat.

"Priya, you don't have to do that. I'll take you home. I want you safe."

"Really? You want me safe? That's a laugh and a half! Save it, Boss! This conversation is over. I don't need to hear all the reasons you liked me, nor do I need a goodbye kiss. I've been wearing my big girl panties for a long time now!" Her chest was heaving with each word she spat out to him.

"So that's it then? We're done?"

"You told me in not so many words that I was just a conquest to you—your words—not mine! So, of course, we are! Thank the Lord! The Uber is here. Goodbye, Boss. I'll see you at work on Monday, but please understand I'm putting out my resume. I'm not sure if I can still work with you. Not after this." Tears were now streaming from her eyes, making him want to hurl.

"I'm sorry!" He reached to cup her cheek, and she pulled back.

"Oh no! And pardon the French I'm about to utter—but fuck no! You don't get to touch me again!"

It was the first time she ever swore since he'd met her, and he hated it. She picked up her bag, turned on her heel, and was gone.

SHE WAS GONE, AND HE NEVER FELT MORE empty than he did now. a pressure in his chest slammed against him, making it hard for him to breathe.

How could I have been so stupid? How could I hurt her like this?

Braden wanted to vomit, something he couldn't do because he wasn't human, but he wanted to. His stomach twisted in knots as visions of sucking her blood flooded his mind. He had to keep away from her. She'd be safer without him, and if she wanted, he'd wipe her memory of him so she wouldn't hurt anymore. He reached for the wine he had opened for the chateaubriand and began drinking right from the bottle. There was no need to pour a glass because he intended to finish every drop. The timer on the oven dinged, and he pulled out the dutch oven from the rack to let the juices set. It looked delicious, but he'd lost his appetite. Once it cooled, he wrapped it up and stuck it in the fridge.

The rest of the evening and the next two days were mostly a blur. Braden was still overwhelmed with the guilt of drinking from her as his alarm filled the room Monday morning. He'd have to face her today and wasn't sure what to say to her. One thing was, in his mind, Braden would tell her the truth no matter what, and if she hated him—so be it. He'd go through with wiping her memory of him with one exception. Braden would provide for her. He'd pay for her condo and find her a new job—but as a head chef. She didn't deserve someone else taking away her thunder.

When he pulled into a parking space at the restaurant, he didn't expect to see Priya sitting in her car. He figured she'd come in with the rest of the crew, and he wouldn't blame her. He was a total dickwad to her. Instead of telling her the truth, he decided to hurt her even more by making her feel like she was just another sexual conquest. The notion had his stomach wrenching as he opened up his car door.

She did the same, and her eyes met his gaze. Her face was sunken in, she had dark circles under her eyes, and her eyes themselves were red and puffy from crying. If he had a beating heart, it would have stopped right there in the parking lot.

"Priya, there is something that I want to talk with

you about. Please head to my office once you are settled."

She let out a huff and crossed her arms.

"Sure, Boss."

The manner in which she said his last name made him wince.

"Can we go back to addressing each other by our first names, please?"

"No. My first name is only used by my friends and family, and you are neither of those, as you made clear Friday. So, from now on, you are Mr. Boss to me, and you will address me as Ms. Pant until I find another job."

"Priya, I'm sorry! I'm so, so sorry! I was a dick, and I figured that out from the minute I said something so awful that I'm not repeating." He said to her as he grasped her shoulders with his palms.

She lowered her head, unable or possibly unwilling to meet his gaze.

"Yeah, I totally agree that you were a dick. If I say apology accepted, can we just drop this and get on with our day? Because if you think I want to be in your office alone, you are batshit crazy. I don't do well with batshit."

"I'm sorry, but you still need to come to my office because there really is something that I need to discuss with you, and it's not about the specials."

"What more could you possibly have to say to me?"

"Plenty! Now, wait here while I disarm the alarm.

Then put your coat and purse away and meet me in my office."

"Fine. Whatever!"

Once he disarmed the alarm, he opened the door to let her in. She stormed past him to the kitchen to put away her things without a forward glance. He deserved it and understood that, but it still cut him deep. He headed for his office and was about to sit down when she stormed in.

"What is it?" She asked as she crossed her arms in front of him.

He walked to shut and lock the door, and her eyes widened.

"Don't you dare lock us in here!"

"I'm doing it, so we aren't disturbed. What I'm about to tell you is very private. No one can know about this. I mean it. You can tell no one, and I'm telling you this because it's the only way to explain my behavior while I apologize to you again. Remember the other night when we talked about the paranormal and how you believe in a lot of it despite what your religion taught you?"

Her brows creased.

"Yes. I remember. Daddy raised me well, but I don't share his faith with everything else. A lot of stuff is too archaic for me to give into. I mean, ghosts exist, and I don't believe that if you come across one, it is automatically a demon. That's just absurd. And the idea that we are the only intelligent life forms in all of the vast universe is another ridiculously archaic ridiculousness. You can put that right up there by telling people that the Earth is flat! But honestly, what does that have to do with Friday and your apology?" Her eyes searched his.

"What I'm about to bring up is important, Priya. Tell me, do you believe that vampires exist?"

Her brow shot up her head at the question.

"I've never given it much thought, to be honest, but I do realize there are people that believe they are real. I think I've heard of some psychic vampires that feed off of another's energy. I watch a ton of those caught on camera shows, and a few of them thought they caught one."

"Well, yes. There's that. Many humans believe they can steal another human's energy, but I'm talking about something far different."

"You mean like Twilight?" She let out a chuckle, and it was the most pleasing sound he'd heard from her since their fight.

"Yes, like Twilight, only a vampire doesn't sparkle in real life."

Priya's eyes widened as a less than humorous chuckle escaped her lips.

"Wait—what?" Her voice trailed slightly, and then she licked her lips before continuing, her gaze still not reaching his. "Your body is generally cool to the touch. You said you hate garlic—so okay? But you eat and drink like a normal human being! I don't understand." Her voice trailed slightly again as her eyes widened some more. "You're asking me all of this because you are a vampire? How can that be? Wait? Do you have a reflection? And if you don't, how do you shave?"

"Yes, Priya. I am a vampire. Garlic is just a silly Hollywood thing, and I just merely hate garlic. I have a reflection—again, another Hollywood thing, too. But I need to know if me telling you I'm a vampire bothers you."

"That depends on whether you plan on biting me or not. I assume you wouldn't be bringing this up if you truly wanted to—I mean—you would have killed me by now if that were the case. I guess? Right?"

He watched the color draining from her face, and her heart began to race. She was terrified of him, and he witnessed her eyes filled with hate and fear all at once. His following statement might send her over the edge, but he had to say it. She needed to hear the truth.

"First, before I answer you, you must understand that purebloods don't kill humans. That's a barbaric practice better left in the past."

He hoped that statement would soften the blow, but then she went off on a tangent he wasn't willing to go down until he told her what he needed to.

"But how do you survive? And, for lack of a better phrase, how do you keep from *vamping out*? I thought all vampires had a craving for human blood?"

"I survive the same as you. I can eat food like any normal human and practice deep breathing to make the humans around me think I'm just a mortal. I may not be human, but my animalistic side isn't all that bad —or at least it wasn't until I met you. Purebloods don't have to drink blood often, but we still need it. Normally when I do need it, it's from the blood of animals. I hunt for my food. But that's not what I wanted to talk about."

"I see. So you do crave my blood?" Priya said as she bit her lip.

"I do, and when we made love?" He screwed his eyes shut and clenched his fists. He drew blood before he continued. The pain wasn't much, but he deserved far worse a fate for hurting her the way he did. "I accidentally drew blood when I was going down on you. I swear, Priya! I swear I didn't mean to! I'm so, so sorry, and I will understand if you hate more for an eternity for this."

His eyes began to fill with a wetness he'd never experienced in all of his immortal life. The water dripped from his eyes and slid down his cheeks.

"Braden, you're bleeding! Don't weep! Please! I'm sorry too! I didn't realize."

Why was she apologizing?

"Priya," He said as he took her hand in both of his before continuing, "I need to know if you can forgive me for what I did. I know I don't deserve it. If you can't, I can wipe your memory of me. But? I ask of one thing and one thing only. I will ensure that you are taken care of. The roof over your head will be paid for outright, and I'll find you a good job as a head chef somewhere else. Say the word, and you will never see me again."

Her brows raised to her hairline.

"Good God! Why would I want that? Why would I ever want to forget you?"

"But I hurt you!"

"Braden," she said as she released her hand from him to palm both of his cheeks. She brushed the blood-stained tears from them both before continuing, "you didn't hurt me. Not even in the slightest now that I know the truth. Please understand that and understand that I'm falling for you and hard. Granted, I can foolishly fall very hard and quick for men that I shouldn't fall for. I made that mistake before, but I know in my heart you are different! You've shown me that you'd never hurt me as Jordan did. And now I know why you are different from all of the other men. I think your pureblood is what makes you more human. Jordan was the monster—not you."

Was he dreaming? Her gaze met his, and the hurt on her face she'd had on Friday and this morning was replaced with love.

"I'm glad you don't see me as a monster, Priya."

She smiled.

"Jordan is more of a monster than you are—trust that. I'm saying this because even though you bit me, you stopped."

"But I drank from you, and I shouldn't have. It's wrong."

"But you stopped! You aren't a monster, Braden. You never could be. I love you, Braden Boss."

"I'm glad you feel the same about me as I do you, even now that I've told you my secret. I love you, too,

Priya. But, you need to understand something. There will have to be some ground rules."

"As long as we can be together, I don't care what the rules are! I love you, and I'm never walking away from you again."

"Okay. And I won't ever turn my back on you or our love again. So? First, before we go on a date, you must allow me the time to hunt. Hunting helps me to control my thirst. I'll also make sure I have a blood supply in the fridge in case our sex becomes too sensual and I need to stop. I don't ever want to hurt you." He said as he tucked a few loose strands of her hair behind her ear. "And last, you must understand that when I date, it's for keeps. You are mine, Priya, and only mine. I cannot share you with another man. I won't."

"Braden, I don't want to share you with another woman either. Since our first date at The Roosevelt Room, I haven't gone out with anyone else. And I don't plan on doing that ever in my future. And as far as hunting goes, that's fine with me." She frowned slightly. "Can you hunt around lunch?"

"Yes, darling, I can—why?" He said as he cupped her face. "I am glad to hear that I am completely yours."

She smiled.

"Good, because I can't go an entire evening without holding you. If we could, I take you out back and kiss you right now. I need you, Braden."

"I can't go another minute without you either, my sweet." He said as he wrapped his arm around her waist and pulled her close to him. "See? I just can't keep my hands off of you." He picked her up and cradled her bridal style in his arms. "We have 40 minutes before the rest of the staff pour in. I think I know of a good way to pass the time."

He carried her out to the back, kissing her the whole way. Once he opened the door to the outside, he placed her feet on the ground and backed her against the wall.

"I'm going to take my time ravaging you." He said as he kissed her jaw, neck, and collarbone. "You are so beautiful, baby, and I want to take my time kissing you. Tonight, though? I will make love to you. Fair enough?" His thumbs circled each of her nipples before he cupped each mound in his hands. The material was thin enough to feel each of her nipples peak with desire, but oh, how he wished the fabric wasn't so constricting. He needed her, and badly.

She let out a soft moan as he took each breast into his mouth and teased each taut peak with his tongue through the material of her blouse. Her back arched, and she wrapped her legs around his waist in response to his touch.

"I want to explore every inch of you, my darling. But sadly, we have to wait for tonight." His finger brushed her thigh before his thick erection pressed against the inside of her thigh.

"I need you inside me now, Braden." She said in a breathy tone.

"I will never expose your private parts to anyone

else. They are mine and mine alone to worship, taste, touch, and gaze upon. No one else is allowed a free show. No one!"

"Then I have an amendment to your dos and don'ts with dating a vampire."

He knew his eyes were darkening. He could see them through Priya's own.

"Then please, tell me of your amendment."

"Well? I'm not keen on anyone seeing your cock. But? If it's in my mouth, they can't see it now, can they?" She was already unzipping his pants and coaxing his dick out of his pants. Before he could protest, she'd already dropped to her knees and began taking in his full length.

"You feel so good, baby. Oh my God!"

His cock was on fire from her sucking and licking. His balls were, too, as she played with them while she shoved his entire length in her mouth. The sensations were too much. He was about to come, and all too quickly. He placed his hands on her shoulders to steady her, but she didn't have it. Her tongue and mouth worked in unison as she bobbed up and then down his dick, her dick. It was clear to him now that she was claiming it as her own to play with whenever she desired.

"Baby, I going come if you aren't careful."

She released his cock from her mouth before she cupped the shaft with one hand and his ball sac with the other.

"And is that such a bad thing?"

"There's something you need to know about vampire purebloods." His voice was almost inaudible, thick with need. He so wanted to come down her throat, but she had to know he was just as human with his seed as any other mortal. She'd have to decide whether or not she wanted to drink him in. If she didn't, he was totally fine with that. No other woman he'd dated in his existence was willing to *go there* with him. He didn't expect Priya to be any different.

"Unless you taste like bananas—which no semen does—I'm game. You should be exquisite. I want to make you come, baby. Let me pleasure you."

"Bananas? You don't like bananas?" He started to laugh and found he couldn't stop. What woman hated eating a fruit that better represented the male anatomy than an eggplant or spicy pepper? Sure, bananas fell a bit short when it came to specifications, and bananas didn't represent inches well—at least as far as his length was concerned. But still? How can a woman hate bananas? They are the best ingredient for his favorite dessert, banana foster.

"Bananas make me gag. But I swallow, and I don't spit, baby. That's the true difference between love and like."

He was familiar with the term, and the jest squeezed his heart, but he didn't need her to do it, even if he desired her to do so. That's when he knew how deeply he cared for her and how much he loved her. Sure he wanted to tell her the truth, and sure he wanted to make sure she led a happy life whether she wanted to be with him or not. But the fact was, he couldn't exist without her.

"I love you, Priya Pant, with all of my heart." He said to hear after she opened her eyes. "We may both have once been bitten in our lives before, but you captured my heart. And this time, I know, it's forever. We are forever."

She palmed his dick again and sucked him so hard he wondered if she would sever the appendage from his lower waist. If she did, he wouldn't care. He was already comfortable with her claiming his dick for herself. The sucking and bobbing were constant, and he went over the edge moaning as she drank his fill in. She pulled from him after he spilled his last drop and met his gaze.

"I'm yours, always."

Epilogue

The Christmas and New Year's holidays were upon them. Priya and Braden were practically living at his place, and by tonight Braden hoped to make their living arrangements more permanent. He hated Priya was living out of a suitcase; she deserved so much more than that. Braden opened his top dresser drawer and pulled out a small box that contained a solitary three-carat cushion diamond set in a French-set Halo diamond band.

"God, I hope she says yes."

He placed the box in his coat pocket and headed over to The Roosevelt Room, the first place they went to together just a couple of months ago.

He slipped inside and was greeted by the hostess.

"Hi, I have a reservation under the name Boss."

"Yes, Mr. Boss. Follow me." She said as she escorted him to the same table that they had the first time they were there. His legs were a bit wobbly when he scooted into the chair. As he was sitting down, Priya came in and slipped into the seat opposite him.

"Sorry, I'm a little late. Traffic's a bitch and a half because of the holiday. Did you order yet?"

"No, I just got here myself. Would you like to share a bottle of wine?"

"That sounds lovely." She said with a smile.

He motioned to the server, and she brought the house red and poured two glasses for them before setting down the bottle. She then placed a mistletoe between both wine goblets.

"It's couple's night since it's Christmas Eve." The server said with a smile before gliding to the next table.

"Priya, there's something I'd like to ask you."

Priya took a quick sip of her wine and placed it back down on the table before responding.

"What's up?"

Braden clasped Priya's hand, reached into his coat pocket, and smiled as he held the box that would change their lives forever. Beads of sweat began to form on his brow, and his mouth went dry.

"What do you think you are going to have?"

Damn it!

He chickened out. He's never been this tongue-tied before.

"I was thinking of the surf and turf for two—that is, if you'd like it."

"That sounds wonderful."

The server soon came over to take their order and placed another mistletoe on the table for them both.

Appetizers, the main course, salad, and desserts, followed by another bottle of wine and a nightcap of cognac. With each course, the server lay a mistletoe out on the table. It was almost midnight, and Braden still hadn't asked her.

"There sure are a lot of mistletoes on this table. I could make a bouquet out of them." She said with a chuckle.

"That sounds like a wonderful idea." He said as he took her hand and placed the box he'd been carrying in his pocket for hours into her palm. Priya raised a brow and sported a wry smile.

"Is this what I think it is?"

"Priya Pant, you taught me what love is and have made me want to be a better man. In all of my existence, I have never loved anyone more. Please do me the extraordinary honor of becoming my wife?"

Priya's eyes teared, and all she could do was choke out her answer.

"Yes, Braden. Yes." She held out her finger for him to slip on the ring. "I love you."

"I love you too, darling. Forever and always."

They reached across the table and kissed to the sound of the bar cheering and whistling their congratulations.

Before You Go...

Do you enjoy the book Midnight & Mistletoe and are looking for more? Sign up for my newsletter, where I offer more fun!

https://www.authoramandakimberley.com/news letter-signup

If You Liked Midnight and Mistletoe You Might Like...

LOVING THE Alpha

Suburban Shifters
&
Celestials Series

USA TODAY BEST SELLING AUTHOR

AMANDA
KIMBERLEY

Loving the Alpha

White Wolf Waya took out a bear turquoise, carved pipe from his pocket, and packed it with a few fresh herbs from a pouch he had been saving for this special occasion. It was rare to have this type of conversation with anyone in the tribal pack, so he wanted it to be memorable. He fumbled a minute under his ceremonial robe, pulled out a lighter, and lit the pipe while taking a few puffs. The earthy-colored herbs turned to several shades of rose and amber. Once satisfied with the vibrant hues that emitted from the pipe, he handed it over to Lenox, who was seated on his right in his study.

"Now, I'm sure this will not come as a surprise, Lenox. The rumors have been buzzing around the tribal packs quicker than a bumblebee. I've asked you here in my study because I'd like to talk about you becoming the chief of the tribe." White Wolf Waya said while patting Lenox on the shoulder.

Lenox's eyes widened as his gaze met White Wolf's. He had an idea this was why the old man summoned Lenox to his home in New York. Rumors had been flying around for weeks that White Wolf wanted to retire. Waya had seen little of the countryside, except the campgrounds they frequented for the PowWows they performed in. But Lenox refused to believe any of it was true until he heard Waya utter the words for himself. Lenox beamed at the old man and then darted his gaze over to the large picture window overlooking the gardens of Waya's home just as heat rushed over his cheeks. The embarrassment of his excitement was getting the best of him. He couldn't show weakness. Certainly not during one of the most important conversations of his life. Overindulgence in any emotion was a major flaw for an alpha.

"There are a lot of our kin tribes here in New England, Lenox, and you'd be great overseeing all of them with Ronan. You are both great Alpha Warriors and would make influential leaders among our people."

Lenox took the last puff of the pipe and almost choked on the smoke when he heard what Waya was proposing.

"I'm sorry. This must be a misunderstanding. What do you mean Ronan and I will oversee the New England states together?"

White Wolf raised his brow as he took a few puffs on the pipe.

"I mean that I'd like you to co-chief with Ronan, so I may retire. This is a big territory to cover, and it is best if there is more than one successor. The job of chief has become complicated over the years. There's a lot more paperwork now that society has become more civilized. I feel it is best to share the burden to lessen the stress. You may split up the territory amongst yourselves, or you may both be co-alphas. I'll leave that to you both. However, it is best to take some pointers from Ronan when dealing with laws forged with local government on sacred land."

"But I am stronger than Ronan. I don't understand why you would not pick me as the soul alpha chief." Lenox said.

He clenched his fists, hoping the pain would help make a semblance of what White Wolf was telling him. No other tribe in either of the Americas had co-chiefs. So, to start now made no sense. Especially since Lenox was a stronger warrior than Ronan. It had been a while since any tribal pack was led into battle. The last time they were, Lenox had been the one leading them. His war tactics were also more genius than Ronan's. Even though the previous decade had been peaceful throughout the tribal packs throughout New England, they were still packs. It took little for one alpha to butt heads with another. This was why Lenox was insistent on tactical training with his warriors daily. Anything less, and they'd be useless in a war.

"Yes, you are powerful. And I don't deny that you are probably physically stronger than Ronan, but you are younger than he is. Ronan's vision with our people is to lead us into an era of peace among all the packs for the next millennia. The tribal packs have never been this peaceful with one another in our history. Ronan has a great vision for us all, and I believe our people are craving peace. Our people will do many beautiful things with your persuasion and his vision.

"It sounds like you're saying that Ronan has the brains, and I have the brawn."

"No, I do not mean that. I am merely saying I'd like you to ease into the position of the chief by having Ronan help you. You are young and have much to learn, Lenox. With Ronan's guidance, I believe you will learn well." White Wolf said as he patted Lenox on the shoulder.

He took another puff from the pipe before continuing.

"Let's have dinner with Ronan and the rest of the elder tribe. My wife has prepared a feast in celebration of today."

Lenox nodded and lowered his gaze. He tried not to let the chief's words sting his badly bruised ego, but it was hard. Even as Waya dangled a beer, the edginess of the conversation was difficult to shake. They both headed into the great room. Various discussions buzzed in Lenox's ears, but his mind clung to the previous one like a wet towel.

How can he think I'm too young? I am the strongest out of anyone in the tribe, and I should be the only alpha.

Lenox looked over at both Ronan and his daughter, Fallon. Their eyes were light. Giddy with the news and celebration. He clenched his fists again, wondering how he would face his son Gavin with this massive blow. Lenox had been practically bragging all week about becoming the chief and made Gavin train harder to prepare for being his beta.

This type of transition would be complex. Lenox and Ronan didn't always see eye to eye. This idea of co-leadership was finalized as far as Waya was concerned. But Lenox was determined to change his mind. As Lenox went over scenarios, fights brewed between him and Ronan in his mind. Every tribal pack discussion seemed to be a significant issue that he mulled over. He cared for Ronan--considered the man a brother. His son Gavin would one day marry Ronan's daughter, Fallon. They were betrothed to each other when they were pups. But through the years, they'd fallen in love on their own. They were soon to be engaged. Ronan was as close to a brother as Lenox would ever know. And, for that sake, he had to at least try to make this work. White Wolf would not likely budge in this co-alpha decision he cooked up unless Lenox tried to meet Waya halfway.

Lenox took another pull from his beer as if the motion would swallow the decision Waya just made for his brother and tribe deep within his subconscious. They were all there to celebrate, and there was little he could do to convince the council otherwise when the pipes and booze were out. Lenox headed over towards the table that displayed snacks. The drive to New York made him famished, and he only just realized the pangs his stomach was giving off when the food was placed out on the long dining table.

He perused the spread, reached for a potato chip, and immersed it in the onion dip next to the overflowing bowl of salty goodness. As he was going for another one, a hand had blocked his arm.

"Lenox! I'm glad you are here! It's great to see you!" Nikiti said.

"It's been a while, old man! How are you and that beautiful family of yours?"

"We are well!"

"Do you plan on making it to Connecticut this year?"

"Probably for the annual Pow Wow in Mashantucket, but not any sooner."

"Send me a text when you head back into town in October."

"I sure will! And congrats on being a co-alpha! You will lead this tribe to greatness. I just know it."

Lenox smiled through the beer bottle he quickly shoved in front of his face. The word co-alpha cut through him like a knife. The pit of his stomach tightened as Nikiti patted his arm again.

I should be the soul alpha!

A rumble grew in Lenox's chest as he clenched his fists again. The sensation from his nails driving into his palms almost felt like he was piercing his skin. It was a desperate attempt on his part to block out his anger. Another hand rested on his shoulder, breaking him from his thoughts.

"Dad, what are you doing?"

"I'm just enjoying the food and a beer. Why Gavin?"

"Because it doesn't seem like you are enjoying yourself. What's the matter? And don't lie. I already know when you do. Your right eye twitches. So it does you no good to tell me different."

"Gavin, go back to your girlfriend and leave me be."

"So you can stew? No. Not a freaking chance in hell, Dad." Gavin said as his gaze locked onto his father's. "This is about Ronan, isn't it?"

"Gavin—"

"Don't Gavin me! Spill!" Gavin said as he directed his father back towards the study.

Gavin placed his drink, and his father's on the dark mahogany desk towards the study's back. A red and ivory Persian rug framed the floor around the desk.

"Dad, I get this will be hard for you, and it's hard for me. You know Ronan wants Fallon to become pack leader with me once you two wind up retiring. Since mom died, you and I haven't exactly had to answer to anyone but each other and our own wishes. But maybe being part of a family unit is exactly what we need? We haven't been moving on very well, and maybe this will help us do so."

"Your brain has turned to mush because of that girl of yours. A family that rules together only works for the humans. We are werewolves, Ronan, and meant to lead the alphas. This is our destiny, and the role of the alpha isn't meant to be shared with anyone, son."

"Bullshit! Fallon is the best thing that ever happened to me, and you know that! She was the only one that was there when Mom died."

"You are out of line, son!"

"No, you are the one that's been out of line for a long time. Dad, I know a part of you died the day she did. I mean, if I ever lost Fallon, I'd probably do the same as you've been doing for the past six years. But Dad, when she died all of those years ago, I didn't just lose her that day. I lost you too."

Lenox took in a breath as he gazed into his son's eyes. When he was younger, they were always a deep verdant green, but now they were a whiskey color, something much more fitting for his maturing thoughts. A smile formed on Lenox's face as he thought about just how wise his son really was. Lenox palmed his son's cheek with one hand and drew his son into his chest to hold him as he used to when he was a pup.

"Oh, son! Leave it to you to lead me in the right direction. I can't say that this co-alpha thing is going to work. But you are right that I should at least try."

He pulled away from his son and reached for the drinks, handing Gavin his. Lenox raised his beer.

"Here's to new beginnings with our family!"

* * *

"Why are you allowing Ronan to treat you like a dog, Lenox?"

Keme grunted as he stomped his foot into the floor to make his aggravation about this territory bullshit well known. He smoothed out some of his light hair and took a pull from his beer.

"I'm not allowing Ronan to do anything to me. He had nothing to do with this decision. All of this is coming from White Wolf Waya. You know that."

"Bullshit! I've discussed this countless times before with the elders. You should be the soul alpha in your tribal pack!"

Keme pounded his fist onto the oak desk in Lenox's office. Lenox's brows furrowed at the sight of Keme's flaring nostrils.

Keme screwed his eyes shut and took a deep breath before continuing. The packs in New Hampshire and Vermont were getting pissy about territory boundaries. This went on for the past two years. Keme was itching for a war to prove he was the soul alpha of both states and Canada. The last battle he had waged on vampires and witches, and the outcome didn't turn out so well, so this seemed like the best chance for him to prove himself among his pack.

"We need strong leadership, and you are the one who can provide that strength. It is imperative, especially now, since our alliance with the vampires is uncertain. I've trusted none of them. Not since Alec and Armand tried to defy nature and bring abominations into this world. Waya has told me I must remain civil. However, I've recently learned that one of them was going against the 14th-century peace treaty. It is my duty to make sure that no one tries to mix magical races. All bloodlines need to remain pure. It's what the gods want."

Keme crossed his arms and let out his chest. He needed Lenox to take him seriously and join in his cause. He wasn't sure if any other packs would go up against the gypsies and the vamps. It was hard enough convincing Conan and Dante to fight them last year, and Keme still had his proverbial tail between his legs after having to retreat from that fight. He didn't expect Zhang to help the vamps and witches' cause. Of course, he probably should have expected it, given the old man's loyalties to lie with witches. He is a sorcerer, and being a distant cousin to witches makes them his only family.

"Heavens Keme! I had no idea! Surely it's just a rumor." Lenox said with widening eyes.

"I don't trust Alec or Dracula as far as I can throw them. Alec's been with a werewitch named Morgan. That union would be fine under normal circumstances, but she's a dire, which means she's got some power behind her. I also believe her to be Obsidian incarnate. Obsidian was a gypsy vampire, and we can't have a child born with a trifecta. I am counting on you to lead your northern New England tribal packs so we can fight against the real evil. See that you become the soul alpha. Ronan is too soft for something like this."

"I'm sure Ronan wouldn't want this happening any more than you. If we talk to Alec—"

"Don't you remember the days of Kate? There is

no reasoning with that vampire, Lenox. Kate was his niece, and he fought us tooth and nail. He nearly wiped out half of the Americas before European settlers discovered the territory. We have to fight fire with fire."

Keme couldn't help but wink and brandish a half-smile. He prayed that bringing up Kate was enough to persuade Lenox into fighting for the alpha position. The tribal packs respected Lenox, meaning Keme would have the backing of all the New England tribal packs at his disposal. He'd not only gain territory, but he'd have a chance to win back Morgan, as well.

Ronan would never help Keme because he felt the treaty had become as rigid as the older wolves in the tribe. He wanted to redraft the pact. Keme believed magicals should only go so far back with genes like humans. He felt only the bloodlines of the magical races in the present life should be considered for unions. Lenox accepted the old ways and feared the gods. He'd fight for the treaty as it stood today.

"But what if I cannot convince White Wolf Waya that I should take the lead?"

Keme's eyes narrowed slightly at the question, and he grunted before responding. Lenox was strong. By him talking like this, it proved Ronan and Waya were turning Lenox into a puppy dog.

"Do you need a nipple to nurse that beer bottle? You are pussy whipped—can't you see that? Those two have clearly made you soft. This isn't how a powerful wolf reacts to what I'm telling you. We can't have half-breeds or a trifecta on our hands any longer. Perhaps you should leave the tribe and train with me. I will toughen you up so you can overpower them both and gain your rightful place in the New England tribal packs. I count on your strength and bravery in this second battle I am facing with the King of the Vlads."

"Alec is here in The States now? I thought he and Lilith were still in England with Dracula?"

"No. Alec came here for revenge against the Rom Baro Gypsy witch Raine and Skye--his soulmate. About a year ago, the whole mess started. I lost our first fight because I only had Conan and Dante backing me. I'm hoping to get stronger and go up against them again, and I sure could use you and your tribal packs by my side on this."

"Are the gypsies going against the treaty, too?" Lenox asked with a gasp. "Because they are human and—"

"No. You need not worry about the witches. But Alec is trying to bed that werewitch, and we cannot have them mate. It goes against our common trifecta law."

"That would be most unfortunate," Lenox said as he shook his head. "I will do my best to convince them of these dangers. If they do not listen, I will take you up on your offer. No werewitch should mate with a vampire. The offspring would truly be an abomination. We cannot have another Kate on our hands." Lenox shook his head again.

"Very well. Keep me posted."

Keme shook Ronan's hand before finishing his beer. Lenox led Keme to the front stoop, where Keme grunted before transforming into wolf form and darted into the thickness of the forest surrounding Lenox's home.

Loving the Alpha
CHAPTER ONE

"What are you doing, Gavin? Good Lord, the sun isn't even up yet. So, what makes you think I want to be?"

"I wanted to spend time with you before the rest of the pack gets up,"

Gavin kissed the tip of Fallon's nose and then buried his head into the crux of her shoulder.

"Well, you better not spend too much time here because you know how our fathers get mad when they catch you in my room. Now scoot so I can go brush my teeth. I hate the idea of you tasting all the death that formed in my mouth overnight."

Fallon flicked her fingers in a shooing motion towards Gavin to get out of her bed.

"I only detect the scent of gardenias from your shampoo."

"Oh my God, you are such a lousy liar!"

She playfully punched him on the shoulder before

tugging on a robe. He caught a glimpse of her perfect mounds in the moonlight that peeked through her thick burgundy curtains just before the robe covered them. But he still didn't take his eyes off of her cleavage as she walked to her master bath. When her pert breasts bounced while she sauntered into the bathroom, he parted his lips slightly and sucked in a breath.

God, she's gorgeous, and if I could, I'd make her mine today. I wish our fathers saw things our way.

Gavin lowered his head and let out a long sigh. This visit wasn't just to steal a few moments with her. It was actually to say goodbye. Not that he could ever bring himself to say the words to her, though. His father wanted to lead his own pack, and he couldn't do that under Fallon's father. He watched her mounds jiggle with each stroke of her brush and then licked his bottom lip when her breasts dipped towards the sink.

He needed to hold her nakedness close to his chest and kiss every inch of her, so he remembered what it was like to love someone. Leaving her would kill him because she is his perfect match, his soul mate in this world. They may have been bequeathed to each other since childhood, but Gavin always understood that the promise of their arranged union didn't matter. He fell for her way before his parents ever discussed the union.

He watched her swig some mouthwash and swish it in around in her full cheeks for a few seconds. The act made for an interesting face, but that's not why it graced Gavin with a wry smile. He thought of her tongue and how delicious it was. Before his father made him leave, he needed one last taste of her. He lowered his head slightly to avoid her gaze as she crawled back into bed with him. He wanted so badly to tell her of his father's plans, but he couldn't. His father had sworn him to secrecy. And since his father was the alpha of their family, he had no choice but to obey.

Pain radiated from his chest cavity. The thought of having to separate from her was too much for him to bear. Every fiber in his body knew how much his absence would crush her, and more than anything he wanted to do was spare her from that pain. The only way he knew how to ease some of that pain was to keep her in the dark until she found the note he had already tucked underneath her pillow.

She slid next to him, and her chest met his. It was the most perfect feeling he's ever known in this life, having such a primal and human connection to Fallon. His hand glided over her bare shoulder and arm under its own accord, tracing each muscle and curve in its wake.

"God, you are beautiful, Fallon." He said as he pressed his lips to hers. His hand snaked up her arm and palmed her cheek as he sucked on her bottom lip. Her essence was exquisite. She didn't have to brush her teeth for him to already understand that about her. But tonight, especially, he was thankful that she did. She wouldn't have enjoyed this last time they would spend together if she was worried about pleasing him. He needed her to relish this last time he had with her. Even if she was unaware it would be.

Her hands reached his torso, and it was only a matter of time before she removed his boxers, so he was as naked as she was. She was truly a girl after his own heart sleeping with only what God gave you. It's not that he wanted to ravish her every second they spent together in bed. No, he was far more attentive than that. He wanted to cherish her, worship her even because she completed him that much.

She had made haste of his boxers before he caught a breath. She straddled over him and thrust his cock inside her. He screwed his eyes shut, trying to ingrain every touch and feel she was freely giving him. He yearned to remember every detail of this moment so he'd remember her, remember their life perfectly.

Her breasts spilled over his chest as she kissed his neck. The sensation was so electrifying that his arms became littered with goosebumps. He let out a guttural growl, greedily taking each mound in his mouth and teasing the peaks with his skillful tongue. She let out a soft moan and laced her fingers in his hair.

The friction her fingertips made while she made small circles on his scalp made him come undone. He continued to thrust himself deep within her willing bits until they both fell into perfect bliss. He stayed in her arms until she fell asleep again. Once she had drifted, he left her bed. He then shifted into wolf form and leaped out of her bedroom window.

The darkness still blanketed the forest when his paws touched the ground. They stung with each step he took away from her because he knew this would be the last time he ever saw her again.

Acknowledgments

There are just too many of you now! So let me start with my bestie Karen.

Karen, you are sometimes "The Wind Beneath My Wings" because you've always been there to lift me up, even through the choppy waters in life. Your calmness in any given situation and your loyalty to listening have always helped me to float above water.

Sarah, my breath of fresh air, my floating line guiding me through everything new in my publishing world: PM—Post Mom. You've been my cheerleader, friend, and confidant in all this new mess I'm searching through in my second wave of life. You've taught me how to gain a sense of inner peace, and I cannot thank you enough for that!

Dale, I love you to death! You've been a beacon, a bestie, and a warrior in this writing business with me. You've reminded me of things I'd long forgotten and showed them to me with fresh eyes. You rock in so many ways for me, and for this, I thank you.

Christie, there are a whole lot of words I can say at this point in our 20-some-odd year climb in this biz! SHH! They don't need the exact year—we are still young in many people's eyes, after all! You've always,

always been a buoy in my life when I've needed you. Either you wind up reaching out to me—or I do you. We've led a very similar path. I'm so grateful for our chats in PMs and on video because it's helped me push through some of the more difficult writing blocks I've had over the years. You've helped me clear my mind so much so that I've got a better bearing on my work. I cannot thank you enough for the weekly talks!

Lastly, I'd like to thank my family that has passed. Mainly my mom, my uncle, which is her twin, and grandma and grandpa. You are all still that lighthouse I look to when navigating through the sometimes murky waters of this life. Thank you all for being there to shape me into the woman I've become.

About the Author

AMANDA KIMBERLEY

USA TODAY BESTSELLING
AUTHOR

USA Today Best Selling and award-winning author Amanda Kimberley has written in various genres in the course of almost four decades.

Her nonfiction blog, which focuses on the chronic disease fibromyalgia, has garnered recognition from various organizations, including Health Magazine. Naming her blog, Fibro and Fabulous, as a top blog for fibro sufferers.

Amanda has also written for medical magazines and sites like FM Aware, The National Fibromyalgia Association's magazine, and ProHealth.

When Kimberley is not writing nonfiction, she enjoys penning romance. Her first Furry United Coalition story, The Turtle and the Hare, earned the 2020 Summer Splash Book Awards of Ink and Scratches for Best Romance. Her Forever Series Books, Forever Friends, and Forever Bound were featured in 2015 and 2016 on the BookCountry website, a division of Penguin/Random House as editor's picks. She has also been featured as a USA Today Happy Ever After Hot List Indie Author with Claiming My Valentine, a Best Poet of the 90's ranking for an anthology, and has had a #1 PNR ranking with Immortal Hunger and Hearts Unleashed.

Amanda Kimberley is a Connecticut native that now lives in the warmth of Northern Texas with her zoo consisting of her husky, tuxedo cat, mice, rabbits, guinea pigs, a tank of fish, two daughters, and a husband.

When she is not writing you can find her cooking whole foods for her pack. She also enjoys reading, hiking, and gaming.

facebook.com/authoramandakimberley

twitter.com/KimberleyLB

instagram.com/amandakimberleylb

bookbub.com/authors/amanda-kimberley

tiktok.com/@amandakimberleylb

Also by Amanda Kimberley

AMANDA
KIMBERLEY

USA TODAY BESTSELLING
AUTHOR

PNR Series

The Forever Series

Forever Friends

Forever Tied

Forever Cherished

Forever Bound

Forever Immortal

Forever Blood

(Coming Soon)

Forever Loved

(Coming Soon)

Forever Yours

(Coming Soon)

Forever Mine

(Coming Soon)

Historical PNR Series
The Witch Journals Series

Salem's Trial by Judge

Salem's Trial by Township

Salem's Trial by Birth

(Coming Soon)

The Gypsy Witch Trials

(Coming Soon)

Colonial Witch Trials

(Coming Soon)

Stand Alone PNR

The Cure

Manifestations

Uncharted

The Pride Within

Co-Author Stand-Alone PNR

By the Pool with Alex Kimberley

Scifi Fantasy PNR
Suburban Shifter & Celestials Series

Loving the Alpha

Loving the Lone Wolf

Loving the Loup-garou

Loving the Rogue

Loving the Lykos

(Coming Soon)

The Equipoise Solar System Series

Laying Claim to the Lion

Laying Claim to the Legacy

Laying Claim to the Original

(Coming Soon)

Laying Claim to the Dragon

(Coming Soon)

Laying Claim to the Leopard

(Coming Soon)

Laying Claim to the Panda

(Coming Soon)

Laying Claim to the Queen

(Coming Soon)

The Pandemic Series

Pandemic Passion

Pandemic Pandemonium

(Coming Soon)

The Midnight Rising Series

Midnight & Mistletoe

Midnight & Magic

(Coming Soon)

Midnight & Memories

(Coming Soon)

Midnight & Mergers

(Coming Soon)

RomCom PNR

The Eve L. Worlds Hellenic Island Shifter Series

The Turtle and the Hare

The Turtle and the Rock

The Ferret and the Fossa

The Leopard and the Llama

(Coming Soon)

Contemporary Romance

The Chronic Collection

Down by the Willow Tree

To Hell With Carpets

Welcome Home

The Chronic Collection

The Just Series

Just Breathe

Just Believe

(Coming Soon)

Just Be

(Coming Soon)

Nonfiction Self Help

The Fibro and Fabulous Series

Fibro and Fabulous: The Book

Fibromyalgia and Sex Can Be a Pain in the Neck

Fibromyalgia and Pregnancy

Poetry

Blue Water Baptism

The Puzzle Called Life

For More Information Please Visit: https://www.bookbub.com/profile/amanda-kimberley

CPSIA information can be obtained
at www.ICGtesting.com
Printed in the USA
LVHW100609051122
732397LV00004B/52